The Right Stuff

Love in Brazen Bay, Volume 2

Brill Harper

Published by Brill Harper, 2019.

This is a work of fiction. Similarities to real people, places, or events are entirely coincidental.

THE RIGHT STUFF

First edition. July 8, 2019.

Copyright © 2019 Brill Harper.

ISBN: 979-8223569985

Written by Brill Harper.

About This Book

After being cleaned out by her bigamist embezzling husband, socially awkward academic Tru Stanhope finds herself with one remaining asset: a dive bar in the podunk town of Brazen Bay. Well, half a bar. The other half is owned by the infuriatingly hot Nash McKendrick. He doesn't want to sell and he really doesn't want his once silent business partner to have anything to do with his one true love—the pub.

Nash liked his solitary life just fine before highbrow and pretentious Tru brought trouble, and her little yappy dog, to darken his door. She may be intellectual, but she knows nothing about the real world and shockingly less about men. He's pretty sure he can handle the mousy little scholar, he just needs to figure out what makes her tick. She's just a woman, after all. And women tend to fall all over themselves around him. He'll just lay on the charm, sweet talk her into doing what he wants, and send her on her way to a life better suited for her so he can get back to his.

But Tru has different ideas. She's tired of the sheltered life she's lived until now. She wants to experience real passion, a real career, and a real purpose in life. And she's decided Nash is going to help her with all three.

Author Confession: Nash could have any woman he wanted, so I deliberately gave him the one he doesn't want. Because authors are evil and I like trouble. I hope you enjoy the opposites attract trope as much as I love writing it.

Chapter One

Gertrude Alise Stanhope Finnegan

I try to focus on the conversation that my friends, Blonde One and Blonde Two, aka Elaine and Marta, are having without me, but all I can concentrate on is the salad dressing stain on my silk blouse. I don't get invited to "ladies who lunch" activities very often, so I think I ought to try harder to fit in, but I have nothing to add to the conversation about the Botox faux pas someone I don't know has been victim of. Someone Elaine and Marta claim doesn't need the Botox as much as she needs dental whitening as they wonder why she didn't start there.

I run my tongue over my own teeth and worry that I've never whitened them. Should I have? There are so many things I don't understand about my world, and I have no excuse. I was born into it, after all. Raised in the same Fifth Avenue penthouse I still live in.

Elaine is getting married to a man I don't remember, but I'm sure I've met since we all graduated in the same class. He didn't stand out, though, and that was mostly because I hadn't been the typical sorority member and didn't have the same college experiences my sisters did. I was only able to attend a few of the mixers and lived off campus all four years. My grandfather had needed me, and I can't regret the time we spent as he battled Alzheimer's. Not even if it meant I had virtually no social life.

"Tru, do you have any words of wisdom for the bride? After all, you've been married for two years," Marta asks, pulling me away from my stain.

"God, yes," Elaine adds. "I love my Michael, but you surprised all of us with your snap wedding to the silver fox. He's so...mature."

Marta smiles "And charming. For real. He's like an American James Bond."

Richard Finnegan is both those things. He takes care of me, stepping in when Grandfather slipped far out of my reach. I'd have been lost without Richard.

Elaine sips her wine. "It's so romantic, really. I never thought of going for an older man, but you wear it well. You've always been ages more mature than the rest of us. I mean that in a good way, of course. But even though we were surprised to hear you'd gotten married, when I saw the likes of him, it all made perfect sense. Normal guys could never do it for you in college, either."

"I wouldn't say that," I argue. "I just never had any experience with dating them. Richard is the only man who talked to me outside of class." I shrug. "It just made sense for us to be together when we were grieving for my grandfather. Richard was like a son to him."

The truth is, most people find me odd. I know that. Richard is the only one who was able to see I'm not a snob...I'm just shy. We were both so distraught when Grandfather started declining so quickly near the end. Richard promised him, during a lucid moment, that he'd make sure I was taken care of. And he has.

"Well, I think it's terribly romantic. What's it like being with an older man?"

My single gold band wedding ring feels very tight today. Richard thought it was a good idea to keep our rings simple, unlike the ring on my other hand that belonged to my grandmother. I know he wishes I wouldn't wear it, but it makes me feel closer to her.

What's it like being married to an older man? "It's lovely, really."

It's *lonely*.

I don't think I said that aloud, but both the women look at me with pity.

I long for something indefinable. The easy camaraderie between Elaine and Marta, who try, bless them, to include me once in a while despite my awkward social skills. I want the catch in Elaine's breath when talking about "her Michael." I never really belonged anywhere. Not with my grandparents, who retired decades before taking me in. Not in high school, when I went home in the afternoons to care for my ailing grandmother. Not in college, when I did the same for my grandfather. Certainly not in my marriage to a man twenty years older and busy, so very busy.

I have what most women dream of—a penthouse apartment, a gentleman husband, more money than I know how to spend. I have friends, at least the kind who invite me to lunch a few times a year, even if I don't feel particularly close to them. I have Fifi, currently napping in her Louis Vuitton pet carrier. My feeling of discontent is an embarrassing display of first world problems.

But if you took away my money, my marriage, and my poetry major, no one would know me. Not the Tru that is under all those things. And the scariest of all, I wouldn't know myself.

After lunch, I do what any bored antisocial socialite would do and shop for things I don't need while continuing to contemplate the things missing from my life that I can't buy at Barney's. I actually hate my wardrobe but find myself buying virtually the same things time after time, and today is no exception. Because, also, I hate shopping. I notice no other woman my age is in the section I'm shopping in, but it's so much calmer in this department. There isn't as much to choose from, and the cuts and styles are all similar. Boring but similar.

Maybe I should ask Richard, again, if I could travel with him. He's warned me that his trips are boring and I'll be happier at home, but since I'm not happy, what could it hurt? Maybe we'd grow closer if we spent more time together. I could explore the cities while he attends meetings, and we could at least have dinner together most nights.

By the time I enter the lobby, my arms laden with shopping bags full of my emptiness, I actually feeling better. My marriage is not a love match, but we care for each other as friends. We have the same temperaments. Maybe it is even time to revisit the baby discussion. Richard was right that I wasn't ready to start a family two years ago, but maybe now is the right time. Maybe sex might even be nice now. Richard and I have separate rooms, and the rare occasions he's home haven't been exactly intimate.

I've only had sex three times. Richard has assured me that my low sex drive is normal and that he is fine with it. I wonder if that's really true. Could we be more if I just tried to be less frigid?

As I enter the classy, if snooty, lobby, my low heels click across the shiny marble floor. I drop my packages at the reception desk and ask for them to be sent up in an hour and then head to the elevator bank, my mind suddenly full of ideas buzzing like bees. I can make changes in my life. Surely having a baby would keep the loneliness at bay. Yes, things are starting to make sense. Finally.

"Mrs. Finnegan," a startled concierge emerges from the elevator as I am about to step in.

"Hello, Mr. Brinkman."

He steps back into the elevator with me. I've never seen the man so flustered. His eyes dart around, refusing to settle, and he pulls the collar away from his throat. "Mrs. Finnegan, I must speak with you."

I hope it isn't about Fifi again. I don't know who isn't picking up after their dog, but it isn't me. "What is it, Mr. Brinkman?"

"There...there are some goings-on in the penthouse."

"Goings-on?" My brows knit together. "What kind of *goings*-on?"

"I don't know rightly what to say..."

The elevator opens, and I notice my apartment door is wide open. Not waiting to hear an explanation, I march across the foyer and into my penthouse. My half-empty penthouse. "What on earth? Mr. Brinkman, I've been robbed."

My mind is still trying to catch up when two men come out of my room carrying a bureau. I'm *still* being robbed? Fifi starts yipping, and I look to Mr. Brinkman for help. Only he looks back with apology but no manly effort to stop the criminals. I should be worried about my safety, but it feels like a dream I'm watching from afar. I pull my phone out, finally remembering to call the police, but Brinkman steadies my arm, pulling me out of the way of the men.

They have the name *Johnson Family Movers* embroidered on their coveralls. What is happening? Why are they moving my things?

"Mrs. Finnegan, I'm so sorry for your misfortune. I have been given leave to let these gentlemen take everything on this list. But rest assured, ma'am, each item they put in their trucks is being accounted for downstairs and not one single thing that isn't on this list will be allowed off our property."

I stare at the paper in his hand. "I don't understand. What is happening?"

"Perhaps you should sit?"

We both look around the room, empty of my furniture and any place suitable for sitting. "Perhaps you should just tell me what I need to know."

"There has been a mix-up, I'm sure. But it appears that your Mr. Finnegan has left behind debts of some magnitude."

"Richard? Left behind? What are you talking about? He's in Munich this week, but he hasn't left behind anything." Inhaling a steadying breath, I count to five before exhaling. This will all be explained. I don't need to panic. Richard will take care of everything.

"Mr. Finnegan never made it to Munich." As if my concierge has suddenly become Mr. Finnegan's personal secretary.

"I spoke to him last night. No, wait, the night before last."

"Yes, well, according to the lawyers, yours and the building's, he was not speaking to you from Munich. Have you spoken to him today?"

I shake my head. "No, not yesterday either." I try to recall anything odd from the conversation from two days ago, but he was perfunctorily polite as always.

"Mrs. Finnegan, your lawyer was here this afternoon. He has left you a message and some paperwork on the counter. I'm regretfully sorry, of course, that I cannot be of more service."

Inside the folder is a list of the things the "movers" are taking and an appointment card for the next morning. The list is court ordered, signed by a judge. None of it makes sense. Where is Richard? Why won't he answer his phone? My eyes hit on the last listed item, and I feel tears for the first time since my grandfather's funeral.

But of course.

My grandmother's ring.

I slide it off my finger and lay it on an end table they haven't taken yet, but surely will. As light glints off the sapphires, I remember my thoughts from lunch. Stripped of my money, my apartment, and my husband, who am I? What will become of me? I may as well not exist.

Nash McKendrick

I'M POLISHING THE SHOT glass in my hand and shaking my head at my old man telling the worst joke in history.

When I roll my eyes, Brandon McKendrick, my esteemed father, slants a look at me and points to his cup for a coffee refill.

"Whatever, Pops." I pour more coffee. I wave the pot at one of my dad's oldest friends. "More coffee, Jake?"

"Sure, son."

The comforting sounds of ESPN pour from the TV above the bar, and I continue polishing glasses while listening to my dad and Jake talk. They don't come to the bar much at night, but they come every morning for coffee. Ironwing, my bar, is named for my dad's rock band from the '80s. Jake played bass, and Pops was lead singer. Man, the sight of my dad wearing Spandex in that damn one-hit wonder video makes me shudder whenever I think about it. Judging by the way women love my old man, he could probably still get away with tight pants, but he's a Levi's kind of guy these days.

"Maybe you should spend less time worrying about my jokes and find a nice girl and settle down. One you can bring home to your old pops."

I roll my eyes. My dad is anything but an "old pops." Ironwing may have only had one album, but they were legendary. At least in Brazen Bay. And maybe the state. Probably the county at the very least. "Old Pops" still gets laid on the regular.

"I told you I'm not settling down, Dad. I like being single."

"What about Stella?"

I catch Jake, Stella's father, frowning at my dad and laugh at his pinched expression. "I love Stella. As a friend. You've heard of those, right?" Stella calls me a "kindred spirit" which has something to do with some girl book she read in middle school about Anne in a green house or something. But there is no heat, no flash between us, and we are both content to let the town assume we will get together eventually because it means they leave us alone more. They give us space to "sow our oats."

I haven't sown with anyone in a while, but my reputation precedes me, helped along by my dad's reputation, which is also more bark than bite. But the McKendricks are the town heartbreakers, despite lack of hearts actually broken.

"Besides, if I start dating Stella, she'll take it as permission to pay her rent late or get a dog or something." She's my upstairs tenant, mostly so I can keep an eye on her. Just not in the way my dad thinks. I'm more of a protective brother. She has one of those already, but if you ask anyone in town, they'll tell you Stella needs more than one.

"I guess I'm never getting grandkids, Jake," Pops laments.

"Heaven help us all when Stella has kids. Her mini-mes are going to terrorize this town," Jake adds ruefully. He's probably going to be a grandpa soon, though. Stella's brother, Leo, is engaged to a librarian most of us didn't even know until recently. Which is saying a lot for Brazen Bay. People here know if you change toilet paper brands.

I take a quick inventory of anything I might be out of on the shelves while I talk. "I'm not marrying Stella, and I'm not having kids, Pops."

I'm saved when my cleaning woman, who's cute but nearly jailbait, comes bounding through the door that separates Ironwing from the stairs to the two apartments.

She has an interesting bounce as she waves and lets herself out. A bounce that all three of us admire for a quiet moment. "How about her?" my dad interrupts my non-thoughts.

"She's a little young, don't you think?" Jake answers before I can, thankfully. Jake has daughters. Consequently, he always sees things a little differently than my dad does.

"She's legal," my horndog dad answers.

"Dad," I warn. "She's still a teenager."

I'm going to harass him some more when I catch sight of a woman pacing the sidewalk outside, the same woman I saw ten minutes ago. She's dressed in the kind of clothes you know are expensive even if you know nothing about women's clothes.

She is obviously lost. And confused. But I have a feeling that she is bad news, and I always trust my gut.

I fold my arms across my chest and watch her pace. There is something I like about her profile as she marches by the window again. The button nose maybe. But still, she's trouble.

I should listen to my gut and sneak out the back door. Let my dad deal with the little miss. For the life of me, I don't understand why I find myself walking to the front door instead.

Maybe what I need is a little bit of trouble.

Chapter Two

Tru

I pause, my hand on the door. Then let it drop again. Honestly, I'm being ridiculous.

It shouldn't be this hard. It's just a door. I've had enough of them slammed in my face over the last six weeks that I know it can't really hurt me.

Physically.

I read the stenciled logo on the window again. *Ironwing*.

Ironwing is a dive bar.

Ironwing is in the middle of nowhere.

Ironwing is the only thing I have left in the world that doesn't fit in my car.

My secondhand car. With a questionable radiator.

I curse my husband...ex-husband...no...*non-husband*...one more time.

I have a lot of questions for Richard. And if I ever find him, I'll be sure to ask: Why did you steal my inheritance? Why did you marry me when you were already married to someone else? Why did you invest 60 percent interest of my money in a dive bar in the middle of nowhere?

Of course, the question that burns my soul every night would go unasked: What is it about me that made me such an easy mark?

Because I don't particularly want to know.

I've never pretended that he loved me. But I always, always thought...no *knew*...that he cared about me. I trusted him with everything—my money, my reputation, my grief. The man fleeced me and humiliated me, but I hurt the worst for my grandfather. My grandfather loved Richard. He left this world assured that I was cared for, my inheritance protected, his good name unsullied. I can accept responsibility for what Richard did to me—it was my own fault for being naive—but I will never, ever, ever forgive what he did to my grandfather's memory with this betrayal. And I will never forget.

The old Tru is dead to me. Never again will I rely on a man to take care of me. Never again will I be naive and uncurious about my own life. I'm not handing the wheel over to anyone ever again.

But I don't pull the door open.

I breathe in the slightly tangy salt air. The middle of nowhere is actually quite pretty here on the water. And quite well fortified with snacks. The cupcake I ate for breakfast was delicious. It's no fault of the baker that I might throw it up.

To the corner and back. That's all I need, and then I'll go in and see what is to be done with the rest of my life now. Yes, once more to the corner and I'll—.

"Are you protesting something?"

I jump out of my skin, whirling around with poor Fifi bouncing around in her carrier. In the doorway, holding the door to the bar open with his back, stands a tall, beastly almost, man. His dark mussed hair looks freshly raked through, and his arms are crossed in front of him in that way men have of looking relaxed even if they aren't. It certainly showcases the way his t-shirt stretches tautly over his shoulders.

And he is handsome. Too handsome.

And that means trouble.

"What would I be protesting?" I ask, determined not to let the slight tilt of his lips fluster me. Let him smirk.

"I don't know, but I'm about to make you a picket sign if you pass by the windows one more time. If I could figure out what you're protesting. Maybe instead you can wear a sandwich board and bring in some customers."

"You work here, then?" I ask.

"I do." He looks me over, top to bottom, assessing me. His gaze feels hot, leaving little trails of warmth over my skin. "Would you care to come in?"

I don't like the way he raised his brow at the end there. He is flirting. I don't have much experience with flirting, but I know when a man is doing it. And I know he couldn't possibly mean it, based on the fact that men who look like him are not interested in women who look like me. Unless they are after my inheritance, of course.

I look around the empty street, unsure of what I'm waiting for. I *do* care to go in. That's why I'm here, after all. But at the same time, I don't want to enter that pub. I don't want to go in more than I have never wanted to do something in my life. Because that will make all of this real.

"I suppose."

He raises his brow at the defeat in my voice.

The interior is dark, which was not surprising. It's not like people need a lot of natural light to drown their problems in a beer. I tried that myself one night. But after two beers, my stomach felt bloated and sour and I couldn't hold onto the fleeting buzz before the headache came. And then all I had were problems and a hangover. Not really worth the price of admission.

The bar itself is glorious. I run my hands over the glossy wood as I take a seat on a stool. Handcrafted. Well cared for. The bar is a piece of art.

There are two older men at the other end of it watching me very closely. I'm glad to see they have coffee cups in front of them and not beer glasses, so I ask for coffee when Sir Smirksalot gets behind the bar.

He leans over the bar toward me, bracing himself on two very sturdy forearms. He's not invading my space, he's edging on it though. My first instinct is to shrink back. But that's old Tru. "Are you sure?" he asks in a very serious tone despite his laughing eyes.

A warm flush spreads through my body. An awareness that I've never felt before about a man spreads that flush lower.

"Yes, I'm sure." I am also sure I'm going to fire him. He's smirking at the customers and second-guessing their drink orders. That can't be good for business.

Although the way his cinnamon eyes flash when he does it might attract more women to the bar.

If they like that kind of thing. I don't. Not really. Not much.

He puts a cup of coffee, creamer, and sugar in front of me. Also a shot glass of something.

"What is this for?"

"You'll see."

My hands shake as I prepare my coffee, but the bartender just watches me while he polishes a glass. I should ask him for information about the owner. Maybe after some caffeine.

I sip gently, hoping it isn't too hot. But then something strange happens. The vile liquid actually attacks my taste buds. It isn't a fair fight. I shudder and push the offending mug away from me in case it comes back for more. My eyes water and bile mixes with my saliva. The bartender pushes the shot glass toward me and I down it quickly. Anything to get rid of that horrible taste.

The alcohol burns as it goes down, and I cough, hoping not to retch because I know beyond a doubt that the coffee would taste even worse on the way back up.

"What *was* that?" I ask when I catch my breath.

"Jet fuel in the white mug. Tequila in the glass."

"Wha—why?"

"I wish I knew. The only people who ever order coffee are those two sitting down there, and they like it for some reason." The men raise their cups to me.

"It was awful. It was more than awful. I majored in poetry, and I can't even think of a way to describe how literally terrifying that coffee was."

"You majored in poetry?"

I stiffen. "Yes."

It seemed a good idea at the time. Funny thing is, my degree isn't very helpful in my current situation. It didn't really prepare me for tax evasion, bigamy, and employment.

He leans over the bar, again not quite in my space, but close. Close enough that I notice his brown eyes are flecked with gold. "What does a poetry major do?"

"Teach. Write. Barista if they can get it."

He smiles in a non-smirk way. He has a dimple. How is that fair?

"Which of those do you do?"

"Nash, more coffee down here!" One of the men yells.

Nash? He is Nash? Well, that settles it. My life has not magically turned around.

"In a minute, you old geezer." He turns his attention back to me. "Now, where was I..."

"You're Nash? Nash McKendrick?" Of course he is. I'd been hoping for an older man. I do better with older men. Well, no. That isn't exactly true.

"Guilty."

I glance down at the customers he is ignoring. "Maybe you should help them?" *And give me time to formulate what I'm going to say because all I have on my mind now is that damn dimple.*

"It's just my dad. He can wait." He nods his head at the men. "Say hi to the nice lady, Dad."

His dad doesn't look old enough to be his dad. But he does look awfully familiar.

"Hi, nice lady," the man says. And then he smiles and my knees weaken a bit. Wow. How do I know that smile? Wait a minute...He is...he is...

"I'll save you some mental gymnastics," Nash says. "That down there is Brandon McKendrick and sitting next to him, Jacob Stone. Formerly of Ironwing, the band. Currently the Cliff and Norm of Ironwing, the pub."

"Your dad is a rock star?" I don't know a lot about current music or rock music in general, but even I recognize the name Ironwing. Why I hadn't put it together earlier, I don't know. I just assumed there really was such a thing as a bird or something called Ironwing.

"Was a rock star. Now he's just a barstool warmer."

"Why?" I look around again. The place doesn't exactly scream "cool."

"He created the name, the bar owner, and handcrafted the actual wood bar. I guess he feels squatter's rights."

I rub my hand along the wood. "It *is* a lovely bar."

"Thank you. We spent a long time on it."

"We?"

"Yeah, Dad and I. There was a time I thought I'd go into woodworking just like him. Instead, I heard the siren's call of the pub."

The pub is a tribute to his father. It is written all over his face. He is proud of his dad. Of the wood bar they handcrafted. Of the pub. I'd really been hoping that Nash McKendrick would be more of an investor like me, with no personal ties to the place. That would make my life much easier. But easy doesn't seem to be in the cards for me lately.

"What's your name, sweetheart? And what brings you to Brazen Bay to picket my establishment?"

Double damn that dimple. And that charm. I hate charming men.

"My name is Tru."

"I like that," he says, leaning on the bar and waiting for me to finish. "And what brings you to Brazen Bay, Tru?" God, he smells like the sea or something. I shake my head.

Don't get distracted, Gertrude.

"I own this bar."

Nash

SO SHE'S A FRUITCAKE.

I back away from the counter, putting distance between myself and the unhinged one.

"Actually, we both know that's not true, Tru," I say carefully. "I own this bar. Me and a sweet little old lady named Gertrude Finnegan."

She raises her delicate hand. "I go by Tru Stanhope. Tru is short for Gertrude, for obvious reasons."

Gertrude Finnegan, my silent partner, suddenly isn't so silent anymore and unease creeps up my spine.

"We've been ...downsizing my properties, and I've come here to maximize the potential of the establishment."

I hold my face very still, trying not to overreact. "How do you get Finnegan from Stanhope?" It isn't my biggest concern, of course, but I need time to think.

She straightens like she suddenly remembers she has a steel spike for a spine. "Stanhope is my maiden name."

My eyes immediately go to her ringless hand. "So where is Mr. Finnegan?"

"He's out of the country. I've looked at the numbers. We need to turn Ironwing into a successful business venture. I can't sell it—"

"Sell it? Wait just a minute here."

"And you can't afford to buy me out, so I am going to fix it."

I balk. It's my bar. Technically she owns 60 percent of it. But it's *my* bar. "What do you know about running a bar, Wordsworth?"

She looks around and shrugs. "How much worse can I do than you are?"

What an uppity little...

"I also own 60 percent of the apartments upstairs. I'll be staying there until we get this place in tip-top condition."

"We have a tenant in #2."

"Then I'll stay in #1."

"I don't think so. I live in #1."

She's trying to act tough. It's not really working. She crosses her arms over her chest, which plumps her breasts up nicely, but doesn't make her look any tougher, if that is what she is after. "It's a two-bedroom. I don't have many personal items. Anymore."

I lean down, get in her space. "I see. You're going to move into *my* apartment. Live with *me*. A man you don't know."

"Should I be afraid of you, Nash?"

Well, I was going to try to intimidate her, but that would be a dick move. Of course she shouldn't be afraid of me. But for fuck's sake. She can't just move in with me.

"I think I'll spend the day settling in to the apartment, and tomorrow we can go over some numbers."

"Listen, lady..." I'm interrupted by the beer distributor and when I look up, my dad is handing her a key from the drawer under the bar. "Dad, no."

She smiles sweetly at him and waves at me before she goes through the door to my house.

Chapter Three

Tru

I cannot believe I just pulled that off. I go upstairs after being assured by Mr. McKendrick, who told me to call him Pops, that Nash would be happy to bring my things up when he was done getting the delivery.

I am sure happy is not the right word for it, but I gave Pops the Popstar my car keys.

The apartment is surprisingly clean, and it's easy to pick out which bedroom belongs to Nash and which is, conveniently for me, already a guest room. Nash's room smells like him. Robust, spicy, a little dark. The guest room smells like Pledge.

I open Fifi's carrier and let her explore the apartment while I try to catch my breath and calm my racing heart.

I have never spoken so decisively to a man before as I did with Nash. I have never just said, "This is what I want and this is how it is, deal with it." But now that my adrenaline is evaporating, I realize I now live with a man. A stranger. A very sexy could-be-dangerous stranger.

I couldn't have imagined the woman I have become two months ago. I'm surprised every day that I'm still here. Still breathing, still fighting, still feeding my dog and breathing air and just living. Nothing in my life experience has prepared me to be broke or deal with business or even people I don't know. I've never stood up to anyone before. I never had to. Now I just barged into this man's life and moved into his house. I am making a pot of coffee in his, our, kitchen, when I hear him enter the apartment and drop my things on the floor.

He stares at me like he didn't expect me to really be here. "The dog has to go."

I shake my head. "Fifi is all I have left."

His eyes soften, but I don't want his pity. "Listen, Gertrude…"

"Tru."

"Tru. This isn't going to work. You know it as well as I do."

"It has to work, Nash. I'm out of options."

He sighs. "I'm going to have my lawyer look over all this, you know."

"You can give your lawyer my lawyer's number. In the meantime, this is where I am staying. With my dog." My heart is racing so fast right now. I can't let him see how scared I am.

"I haven't had a roommate since college."

I lift one shoulder in a half-shrug. "I don't intend to get in your way. I plan to go to business school by the fall."

"It's barely spring."

"The sooner we sell, the sooner I'll be gone."

His gaze narrows and that square jaw lifts toward me. "I'm not selling Ironwing."

"We'll see."

"Woman—" Fifi growls at him when he raises his voice to me. "Easy, Cujo. My blood pressure is in more danger than your mom."

I pick her up. "She's had a rough couple of months."

"Oh, she has?" he asks, knowing I'm talking for the both of us. He takes a step toward us, and I back up. He cocks his head. "You don't trust me to pet your dog? You're going to live with someone you don't trust to pet your dog?"

I swallow hard when he makes another approach. He scratches Fifi behind the ears and I make the mistake of inhaling that pure masculine scent that probably lures mermaids to their death instead of the other way around. My God, my toes curl so hard in my shoes that I have to keep reminding myself that I'm frigid.

"Everything okay, Gertrude?" he asks in a low, teasing voice as my dog melts against his hand. Can he tell that I'm out of breath around him? That he makes me dizzy? He smiles, throwing me further at sea. His eyes, when they land on mine, are hard to read. He slides his hand down to my wrist, rubbing his thumb over my wild pulse. "You seem a little wired."

I slide my wrist out from his grip. "It must be the jet fuel from downstairs."

His lips kick up on one side. "Look, I need to get to the bar. You can stay here tonight, but we need to talk about your plans. You can't just move into my house."

"Our house. It's more mine than yours. You can't make me leave."

He holds up his hands in surrender. "We'll talk later." He's doing well controlling his temper. When he walks away from me, I study the way his butt fills out his jeans and find myself blushing. I'm really incorrigible.

It doesn't take me long to unpack. My lemon-fresh room is comfortable. The quilt on the bed handmade in a star pattern of pastels, the curtains a creamy lace, and the dresser empty. The only thing in the closet is a suitcase.

I check out the rest of the place. I don't think he spends a lot of time here. It's all very utilitarian in the living room, kitchen, and bathroom. So different from the dark antiques I'm accustomed to. I take another peek into his bedroom. That's a little more like him. Maybe just because it smells like him. The room is done in navy and gray, and there are a few framed photos on the dresser. Without stepping in and really making a nuisance of myself, I can't make them out. One looks like Nash and his dad with a fish.

It doesn't take long for me to feel restless, so I go back down the stairs into Ironwing, Fifi in tow.

There's nobody at the bar or any of the tables. Nash is standing at the bar reading a newspaper. He startles when I clear my throat.

"I was hoping you were a psychotic episode. Yet, here you are."

I send him a small smile, hoping I can start off on a better foot. "Here I am."

Two men come in wearing BBFD t-shirts. Firefighters. Is that normal here? For first responders to hang out in a bar just past noon?

"How was your shift?" Nash asks them in a friendly tone, obviously used to the regulars.

"Quiet. Cap is still out on injury, and his replacement doesn't work us as hard on drills."

"Don't tell Leo that or he'll come back to work too soon."

"We're going to practice darts—send us a pitcher, yeah?"

Nash nods and looks at me hiding in the shadows. "You ready for your first lesson?"

"Aren't they working? Should they be drinking?"

"They're off shift. They're all good guys who work hard. We don't give people a hard time for having a beer after work. That's how we make our living, remember?"

I nod. "I apologize. I haven't spent much time in a bar before."

"Really?" he asks dryly. "You ready to learn how to pour?"

"Even I can handle that. Don't you just pull the lever?"

He scoffs. "It's an art. If you do it wrong, it will over- or under-foam. Come here."

I set Fifi's carrier down and let him position me in front of the tap. He puts a glass in my hand but holds his hand over mine. "You want this glass at a forty-five-degree angle about an inch below the tap." He's standing behind me, and I can feel the heat of him, his breath at my temple as he adjusts my wrist to the correct angle. My belly quivers as I try to concentrate on his words and not his potent masculine power. He takes my other hand in his and moves it to the tap handle. "We're going to quickly pull it forward to open the flow of beer. Never open it only partway."

"Why?"

"It will over-foam. It's either on or off. Never between. Got that?"

I nod and find myself sucking in my stomach. This is ridiculous.

"Once it's open, we're going to let the beer flow down the side of the glass until it's half full. Keep the glass at forty-five-degrees and don't let the spout touch the glass. Once it's half full, continue pouring while you gently tilt the glass upright and pour down the center to create about one inch of head."

His low voice in my ear is vibrating in places that make me tingle. I have to resist the urge to lean back against his chest. It would feel so good, all that strength supporting me for a change. I need to get it together.

"So I can start?"

"No. Don't be impatient." Did he just sniff me? I think he just sniffed me. "Once the pour is done with the right amount of foam, quickly turn the tap off. Now you can try it."

It didn't look hard, but the beer foams more than one inch. My shoulders slump. "I screwed it up. Do I pour the foam off?"

"Hey, don't be so hard on yourself. Just let it rest until the head calms down and finish your pour. It will be fine."

While I wait, I angle my head so I can talk to him. "Thank you for not yelling or getting mad. I promise I'll figure it out."

His brow wrinkles up. "It's just beer, Dickinson."

I nod, and duck my head, afraid I'll show that my eyes are starting to well up.

"Hey." He nudges my temple with his nose. "I'd be better off letting you be afraid of me, but I don't sweat the small stuff. And I don't yell at people when they are learning a new skill. Now let's finish this beer."

I swallow hard and nod again. He's actually been really nice considering I've just turned his life upside down.

When he's satisfied that I can fill a couple glasses, he gives me a pitcher and steers me to a different tap, one with more expensive beer in it. "Never let the tap come in contact with the glass or the beer." He takes his hand off mine holding the glass and settles it on my hip. I draw in a shocked breath but pour a flawless pitcher and even take it to the guys playing darts.

A woman wearing a navy-blue dress dotted with white anchors comes in holding a paper bag with grease stains on it, already talking as if in mid-conversation. "They were out of onions, Nash. Tell your patrons they can thank me later when you breathe on them..." She gets to the bar and cocks her head, examining me, then examining Nash. "New employee?" she asks Nash, setting down a heavenly smelling lunch. "Hi, I'm Stella."

I open my mouth to introduce myself and Fifi yips. Probably smelling the food.

"Oh, hell," Nash mutters as Stella's face transforms into what I can only describe as pure joy. "You got a dog!" She rounds the bar and zeroes in on Fifi's carrier. "Oh my God, Nash. It's about time. Oh, he's adorable."

"Not my dog," he says, but I don't think she heard him as she gets down on the floor and starts making baby talk to my dog.

"Who's a good baby? Look at you."

Nash reaches a beleaguered arm down to bring Stella back up. "Not my dog. And no, you can't have one in the apartment either."

Her face falls and she brushes off her dress. I wish I could pull off that kind of style. The neckline looks like she stepped out of a Hollywood movie set in the '50s. Bombshell starlet. Matching shoes. Ruby red lipstick.

So this is his type? It makes sense, I guess. A woman would have to be sure of herself and filled to the brim with je ne sais quoi to keep up with him.

I'm trying to figure out why he didn't tell me a woman lived with him when he introduces me to her. She's going to be a little upset, I'm sure. Even if she does like dogs. Maybe sleeping in my car isn't so bad after all.

The niggle of disappointment surprises me even more than the woman, though. Why had I assumed he was single? Why do I want him to be single? I don't, do I?

"Stella, meet my business partner, Gertrude Finnegan."

"Tru Stanhope," I correct, holding out my hand.

She shakes it briskly and smiles so genuinely I feel warm all over. Which makes me feel even worse that I was even minutely attracted to her boyfriend. "Hi, Tru. Nash told me his silent partner was a little old woman in New York."

"I've been told I'm mature for my age."

"So you're my landlady."

"I...am I?"

Nash is watching my face closely. Too closely. Like he senses my near brush with jealousy. Which is impossible. "Stella rents the apartment across the hall from us."

"Us?" Stella asks, clearly surprised. "There's an us?" She points to me, then to Nash, then makes some gesture with her hands poking one finger into a hole she made with the other.

Nash grimaces and grabs her hands to stop the lewd gesture. "Just for that, I'm raising your rent." She laughs, and he tries to regain his cool. "Tru is utilizing the guest room at my place while she learns a little more about the business. She won't be staying long."

God willing.

"Tru, can I meet your dog, please? I work for the vet down the block and run a foster program for rescue animals."

Nash exhales loudly and sort of stomps away while I get Fifi out. She goes right to Stella like they are old friends. "Nash, your lunch is getting cold," she yells at him across the bar, but he growls at her and does something to the dartboard to reset it.

"Actually, I already heard you were here. My dad called me at work after he left this morning and filled me in. I was just hoping to get more gossip."

"Your dad..."

"The assless chaps one from the band. Nash's dad just wore leather pants and spandex. Mine also had a perm. He taught me how to do eyeliner in the seventh grade because my mom is hopeless with makeup and my sister thinks eyeliner is trashy and wouldn't help me."

I'm at a loss for how to reply to that. Assless chaps? I was just going to ask her if her dad was the one Nash called Jake. "Your dad seemed pretty conservative this morning."

"Oh, yeah. He only ever wears dad clothes these days. So how long are you staying upstairs?"

"I'm going to start business school this fall, so just long enough to learn the ins and outs. I thought it would be prudent to take a more hands-on approach with some of my investments."

She worries her bottom lip and glances at Nash, nodding. "Well, we're happy to have a city girl in town. You can give us some sorely needed cosmopolitan culture."

I look down at my bland outfit, the way it makes me look boxy and sixty. "I think you probably have a better handle on that than I do. I really like your dress."

She beams at me and kisses my dog's head. "Thank you! It has pockets."

Nash joins us at the bar, grumpily, but opens the bag. "Do you like grinders, Gertrude?"

"I don't want to intrude on your lunch."

"Sure you do," Stella answers. "You can have half mine."

I stammer and try to get out of it. But Nash suggests I pour us all an IPA and they divide their sandwiches among the three of us. Stella eats with Fifi on her lap and I can't help but get caught up in their easy friendship. I'm a world away from Tavern on the Green and my ladies who lunch days, but I'm oddly at ease.

"Can I read your palm?" Stella asks holding out her hand for mine.

Nash pushes it away. "You don't read palms. And you do this with every girlfriend I've ever had, making up some bullshit about her love line. Knock it off."

"Girlfriend, huh?" Stella smiles and takes a bite of her sandwich.

Nash narrows his eyes at her, and she kicks him under the table.

I wish I had that kind of rapport with someone, so I don't even mind that she's using me to get his goat.

Chapter Four

Nash

I don't know how I forget, but I walk into my apartment tonight expecting it to be the same as it always is, only just as I let the door close behind me, Tru is coming out of the bathroom wrapped in a towel.

I no longer live alone.

My roommate turns me on.

It's not hard to imagine her in the shower instead of out of it. Her body, sleek and wet, as soap runs down her breasts...

"Oh," she breathes and stops abruptly. Maybe she forgot she didn't live alone too.

I like the catch in her breath. It sounds close to a whimper, and suddenly, I'm filled with longing to hear her whimper and sigh in my arms instead of across the room. I'm pretty sure that's not a thing that is going to happen. Even if she were on board, it would complicate things unnecessarily.

Or would it? Maybe she'd be less frustrating and troublesome if I could soften her with sex. She's a little skittish, but it's not like I didn't see her watching me all night at the bar. Wanting me maybe.

She definitely gets tongue-tied when I flirt with her. Which is fascinating. Like a blushing virgin, though she was married for two years. My gaze lingers over her body a little too long, thinking about how easy it would be for that towel to flick open, and she turns a pretty pink all over.

"You're blushing."

"Just got out of the hot shower." The air thickens between us. "I should get dressed, excuse me."

She brushes past me, and I watch her all the way to the guest room before I let out a long breath. My mind goes back to teaching her how to pull a draft today. Her soft curves, the smell of her shampoo. My first impression wasn't wrong this morning. She's trouble.

The dog wanders past me and scratches at the door. I ignore it. It scratches again.

There's a leash next to Tru's keys, a little pink thing that looks like you could walk a guinea pig with it. I suppose that belongs to Fifi, who is more rodent than dog. Don't ask me why I put the leash on it, carry it down the stairs, and wander the grass in front of my building while it does its business. I am disgusted with myself.

This is not a good way to get rid of it and its owner. Since Tru turned my life upside down this morning, I don't think I've done anything right. I should have been meaner. I should have called my lawyer. I should have refused her entry to my house and my bar. Instead, I practically offered turndown service and now I'm walking her pet rat.

I carry the damn thing back up the stairs too. It's a lot of stairs and rats have short legs. I tell myself I just didn't want to wait while it took too long, but when it licks my face, I know I'm not fooling myself or the dog.

I open the door to a smoke-filled apartment.

"Sorry," she yells, frantically waving a dishtowel below the alarm. "I was trying to do something nice, since you were walking my dog, and thought I'd make us something to eat, but as usual, I'm not good at much of anything."

I shouldn't tell her she's good at making me hard. That's not going to make her feel better. I can't stop staring at the patch of skin between the bottom of her t-shirt and the pajama pants she's wearing. It's hardly the most erotic thing I've ever seen, but try telling that to my dick. "I bet you got a 4.0 in all your literature classes."

She stops the towel and looks at me quizzically. "What does that have to do with burning food?"

"You said you weren't good at anything. I say you're good at poems or whatever." I study her face before she turns away. I don't think she likes being seen. I move in and turn on the fan above the stove. "Get the bread out, I'll make us grilled cheese."

"You don't have to—"

"Just get the bread." I make for a light tone, "So, not much of a cook, huh?"

She shakes her head, watching me very carefully like she's going to have to take a test on grilled cheese later. "Growing up, we had a cook. After my grandfather died, I found someone who would come once a week and prepare meals for the whole week."

She grew up with a cook. She's richer than I thought. I just don't understand where her money went. If she came from that kind of background, why is she sniffing around my bar? "And your husband?"

"Ex-husband." She looks down, her lashes sweeping low. "I don't think he cooks, but I didn't know him as well as I thought I did."

There's a story there. One that makes her shoulders round and her voice go soft. She's vulnerable and hates it. It makes a man want to step up and fix things for her.

Where the hell did that come from? The very last thing I want to do is be some woman's knight in shining armor. I learned what happens to that guy from watching my mom roll over my dad too many times.

But I don't think she has anyone to talk to, and my whole life, I've never not had anyone to talk to. Whether I wanted to talk or not.

"What happened?" I ask casually, looking at the pan and not her. I learned that from my dad too. He told me after I was grown that the key to getting your kids to talk was not looking directly at them during a big discussion. Which explains why he used to take me for long drives when I hit puberty. It worked. I spilled a lot of shit to my dad over the years while sitting in the passenger seat.

"Do you need any help?" she asks, avoiding my question.

I flip the sandwich. "No, I got this." She's trembling. Fuck. I set the spatula down, suddenly filled with a dangerous rage. "Did he hurt you?"

Tru looks up, surprised. "Not that way." She gets out a couple of plates. "We just weren't a good fit."

There's more. *Keep talking, sweetheart.*

"Is he the reason you don't have any money?"

She bites her lip, and I stifle a groan. Why is that sexy?

"That's really none of your business."

I plate the sandwiches and try not to take offense, but it's hard not to. "I think you owe me some answers."

That lower lip trembles, but then she straightens her spine and carries her plate to the couch. "I don't want you to know how pathetic I am."

"Why do you think you're pathetic?"

"Because I am! Richard was a con artist. He got close to my grandfather while he was dying and then...got close to me. He never loved me. He was actually never even married to me. He's in the Caymans now, probably with his real wife and my inheritance. The only thing left after selling everything to pay the back taxes and debt was Ironwing."

I set my plate down on the coffee table so I don't throw it. "That fucker."

She blinks her surprise at me. "I'm the stupid one who married him."

"Tru, it doesn't take long in your presence to realize you have a kind of...innocence."

"Stupidity."

"Innocence. You're trusting, and I'm sure you're very book smart, but I'm guessing your time in the stacks of your ivy league school didn't really prepare you for some of the stuff life has thrown at you. Your ex is a dick. He took advantage of you."

"Well, it won't happen again. I thought...the way he took care of me...all my life, I thought men would take care of me. That's how I was raised. My grandparents loved me, but they brought me up in a way that I would always rely on someone else. But there is no one else. There is only me."

I think about my mom and how she thought men were there to take care of her too.

"So why business school? Why is that so important to you?"

"Isn't that what men do to show they're serious? The world respects businesspeople. They don't respect poets."

"And that's what you want? Respect?"

"I want never to be taken for a fool again. Yes, I want respect." She's practically grinding her teeth. "Tomorrow, I'm looking at the books."

Now she's set my teeth on edge. "Respect goes both ways, Robert Frost. Try to remember I'm not the asshole who took you for every penny you had while you pull the rug out from under my life, yeah?"

I slam the door of my bedroom like a sullen teenage girl. She makes me crazy and I've known her for less than a day. I make it a practice to never be angry or emotional about things—life is easier when you just take it as it comes. This poet with more control of my business than I have is going to have to go.

Tru

I'VE BEEN HERE FOR three weeks now, meshing myself into the rhythm of Nash's life whether he likes it or not. Every day, I'm surprised not to find my things on the curb. Every day, he tells me something about having his lawyer look over things, or we'll work on fixing the place up later, or he's thinking of a way to buy me out.

Every day, we do the same as the last. We eat, we work, we watch some interminable sports program on the television. The bar runs itself. He closes early every night. He has no patience for drunk people. I don't understand why people keep coming. I do understand why it doesn't make more than it needs to keep the doors open—but Nash is reluctant to do anything about it.

He likes Ironwing the way it is. And if I didn't need to figure out how to get out of here, I'd like how it is too.

It's a slow evening, so I brought my textbooks for next semester downstairs with me. I haven't actually been accepted into the program yet, but I figure getting a head start can't hurt. Nash is pretending to polish a glass, but I can feel him looking at me. I try to ignore him while I take an inventory of all the ways I'm not ignoring him. His scent, I'm not ignoring that. It's alluring and sexy, and I know for a fact he doesn't use cologne. It's all him. It's powerful and virile and all the things I never thought I liked. The undertones are bone-meltingly good and zing me in all the places I ought not to be zinging if I value my pride.

I also don't ignore the weight of his stare. It presses on me like he's always trying to uncover something more. Like my secret shame is somehow up for grabs.

And then there's the energy around him that I can't ignore. It's like a swirling vortex of...no...actually, it's like a bug light. It attracts me even though I know it will zap me if I go anywhere near it.

Finally, unable to deny him any longer, I look up at him from my book.

He searches my gaze for a minute, but I don't know what he's looking for. "You can't learn life from books."

Books are safer than men. "Of course you can."

He winks at me, possibly knowing it will cause an all-out body tingle for me. "Tell me what your degree in poetry has done for you. What real-world skill have you acquired?"

I don't want to be a loser. I don't want to be the butt of a joke or the mark of someone's con. It's true, my degree has been useless in many real-world situations, but there is one thing that a degree in poetry has given me.

I know how to rhyme.

I take off my reading glasses and stand up. He pulls back, wondering what I'm up to, and I walk to a table and pull out a chair. As I start to climb on it, Nash rushes over to hold my arm and stabilize my climb.

"What the hell are you doing, Gertrude?"

I rise to my feet, and all seven patrons look at me when I yell out, "Excuse me, I have something to say."

The volume on the jukebox magically goes down, something I still haven't figured out how to do even though I've fiddled with every button on it, and I take a deep breath. "There once was a princess from the city. One day, her life got very shitty. She moved to the Bay, the beast said she couldn't stay, and now everyone has his pity."

Everyone claps and I mock bow, pleased with myself for doing something so unTru. When they ask for another, I blush but do my best.

"The once was a fellow named Nash. Who claimed he had the best ass. It's not what you thought, not supple or taut, but brays too much and eats grass."

Nash folds his arms over his chest. His very broad chest that is stretching the limits of his Hanes t-shirt. He's pretending to be chagrined with me, but I see the smile behind the smirk and I think I just impressed him a little.

He offers me a hand down, but when I get to the floor, he doesn't move back right away, and the chair is pressed up against my legs. My stomach quivers and my nipples perk up like they think they can reach him if they try hard enough. I move my eyes up, way up, and he looks so big and bad and ...sexy. The breath catches in my throat. I can't touch the bottom here. I don't know what to do with sexy. No one has ever been sexy in my vicinity before. His gaze is amused and heated, like he knows exactly what he's doing to me and isn't the least bit sorry about it.

"Ahem," a woman clears her throat from behind Nash, and he turns and steps away.

"Stella," he intones. The way he might to a little sister who is asking to play with his toys or hang out in his "boys only" treehouse.

"I want to borrow Tru for a bit. She hasn't met Dixie, and I think she needs a break."

He puts his hands on his hips, drawing my attention to the V of his waist. "She hasn't been working hard enough to need a break." His gaze meets mine, relaxed despite his pretend gruffness.

"Good, then you don't need her."

"No dogs, Stella. I'm serious."

I don't know why he bothers with the pretend gruffness. I haven't seen it work on anyone yet.

Stella pulls me away to the corner and introduces me to Dixie, her soon to be sister-in-law.

"So you're getting married," I say and bite my tongue so I don't warn her to do a title search on the groom first. "How did you meet Stella's brother?"

"Oh, you're gonna love this," Stella interrupts. "Dixie was a wrong number text to Leo and they fell in love."

"In a text?"

Dixie laughs. "Not just one text, no. Leo flirted with me in the text."

"Gross," Stella interjects, taking a sip of her wine.

"And then we just kept talking."

"Talking." Stella huffs indignantly and good-naturedly. "They had dirty, dirty phone sex and then found out they lived three blocks away from each other."

"Wow, that's quite a coincidence."

"That's destiny," Dixie answers on a sigh. A sigh that says she might actually prefer Leo's company to ours right now.

I roll my eyes and catch Stella doing the same and discover a woman I might actually be able to be friends with in a way I never could with my sorority sisters.

Stella clinks my glass. "I was thinking. I think Fifi needs a friend. You're going to be busy learning the bar business and then school. It would be good for her to have a dog companion so she doesn't get lonely or bored." Stella leans across the table conspiratorially. "I know these things because I work for a vet."

"You're a receptionist," Dixie reminds her.

"I still know what I'm talking about."

Fifi is currently behind the bar with Nash right now. They are both watching the game. I don't know what game. I can't keep them all straight. But Fifi likes to watch the action on the screen, something I never knew she liked until we moved here. "I can't take care of two dogs right now."

"Nash could use a dog."

Dixie looks over her shoulder. "It looks like Nash has a dog."

I shrug, trying not to feel a little hurt that Fifi likes him so well. "We'll be leaving in a few months."

Stella claps her hands together. "Then I shall start working on this immediately. No, actually, the moon is void of course until tomorrow morning. I'll do it after. Void moon is terrible for dog matching."

"What is void moon?" Dixie asks.

Stella's eyes light up. She must really like the moon. "So, you guys know the moon has phases, right? Full moon, new moon, waxing and waning." We nod. "Well, she also moves through each zodiac sign. Void of Course means she's transitioning in the sky between signs—but isn't in either. It's a really good time to do self-care and inner work, but I try not to match anything or sell anything too hard during a void moon. Things just lack oomph."

"That's interesting. I don't know much about moon phases, but I know my grandfather got a lot more restless during a full moon the last few months." They both pat my arms and I'm overcome by the reassuring touch. Touch is not something I've had a lot of in my life. I don't want to cry or garner their pity. "Anyway, I don't think Nash wants a dog."

"Nash doesn't always know what's good for him. That's why it's a good thing he's got me for a friend."

Nash wanders over about ten minutes later. "Last call, ladies."

"Dude," Stella looks at her phone, "It's 8:30. What kind of bar closes at 8:30?"

"I need my beauty rest," he tells her and starts picking up chairs.

"Well, that's certainly true. But still, you could hire actual people to work and keep the place open until a reasonable time."

He picks up her glass. "You done with this?"

I push away from the table, saying goodbye, and go get the broom. While I sweep, Nash does the other closing procedures. I turn off ESPN and turn the radio on. A Frank Sinatra song comes on, and memories of my grandfather make me smile. A kind of watery smile, but it's good to remember him. Boy, did he love Frank Sinatra.

Nash takes my broom, and I'm suddenly whisked into his arms. He starts dancing me around the tables, and I stiffen for just a moment before I relax, cotillion practice coming back to me. "Where did you learn to dance like this?"

"My high school football coach made us take ballroom dancing lessons in the off season."

"That's amazing."

He shrugs. "It's really good for coordination."

I don't think he needs any help with coordination. He seems to know how to use his hands and his body, and dancing is making me think of the kind of sex I've never had. The kind I didn't think I ever wanted. The kind that his arrogance and good looks probably excel at.

He flashes me a smile. A simply devastating smile. "Are you thinking naughty thoughts right now, Gertrude?"

"I don't have naughty thoughts."

"I somehow doubt that is true."

I shake my head. "I'm not like most women my age. I never have been."

"What is that supposed to mean?"

I exhale loudly. I really don't want to have this conversation with him. But maybe it's best to just get it out there. "I'm just not sexual."

He snorts on a laugh. "Sure you are." I try to pull out from his embrace, mortified that he's laughing at me, but he tightens his arms. "Did someone tell you that you shouldn't be sexual?"

"I'm just not."

He pulls me in closer, lowering his head so his strong jaw brushes against my head. In a voice so deep it should be illegal, he says my name. I pull back and look up at him, and our gazes lock and hold. We stop swaying to the music and somehow my heartbeat slows even while my pulse races.

A warm flush spreads through my body again, and I panic. "I have to go."

His loose expression tightens, and he lets go of me and steps back. "Where you running to now?"

My thoughts jumble into a mix of unintelligible gibberish. I don't want him to touch me. I don't want him to let go of me. "I just...I can't...I have to go."

And run I do. All the way up the stairs to *his* apartment. My refuge and the lion's den.

Chapter Five

Nash

Tru has been avoiding me most of the day, which doesn't surprise me, and I'd like to say it doesn't bother me but it does.

Something has her spooked about men, though I guess finding out your husband is a lying thief could do that to a person. But I feel like there's more to the story.

Despite her assurances that she's not a sexual person, I feel the chemistry between us and I know she does too. How could she not? It's enough to set off the smoke alarms faster than her cooking.

My dad brought a pizza over, so we're having a slice at the bar when he whistles under his breath. I know that whistle, so I follow his gaze to the door.

There's a redhead, though the first thing I notice about her isn't her hair color. It's not like she's trying to hide that rack from anyone. She struts in on heels so high she must fight off nosebleeds. The dress that barely covers her is leopard print, and she's got bangles up and down both arms.

The aura of sex surrounding her is potent, stunning almost. She's the kind of woman men fall all over themselves to get near even if they think she's out of their league.

My dad, the dirty old man, is instantly in his version of love.

"What is a beautiful woman like you doing in a dump like this?" he asks when she makes her way up to the bar.

"Seriously, Dad?"

She smiles and runs a long fingernail down his shirt. And then she blinks. "Well, fuck me, you're Brandon McKendrick."

Dad just laughs, used to the reaction. "I am. You're too young to be a fan, though."

"I've got ears, don't I? I didn't realize when I came into Ironwing, I'd actually meet *Ironwing*."

My dad gestures to the empty bar stool next to him. "What can I get you to drink?"

She slides onto her barstool, avoiding a show somehow, and orders a glass of red. Of course, my dad is not paying for her drink, I am. That's how it works around here. But I don't think she wandered in off the street for a glass of wine, so I pay close attention to this Jessica Rabbit newcomer.

"What's your name, sweetheart?" he asks her.

The feline smile that crosses her face promises him the kind of rewards a son doesn't want to think of his father reaping. Just because I've seen him in Spandex doesn't mean I'm immune to more embarrassment. "I'm Pauline. I'm actually looking for a friend of mine. I heard she was in town. Her name is Tru."

I slide the glass to her, my ears perking up. "You're a friend of Tru?" I try to keep the surprise out of my tone, but don't do a very good job.

She raises one brow, chastising me for my misstep.

"We're acquaintances. Is she around?"

It's not my place to question her, but I don't have a great feeling about this. Tru's already been chewed up and spit out by someone who played a different game than she was ready for. Pauline's rules are not PG-rated from where I'm standing. Too late, I notice Tru come through the door with a tower of books in her hands and a dog carrier hanging off her arm.

She's wearing jeans, for a change, but she's paired them with a top that buttons all the way up to her throat with a schoolmarm bow tied right there in case one comes undone. She's wearing her reading glasses, but since she's not reading, she has to look over the top of them to see where she's going. She bobbles the stack until she gets it set down on the bar, and I swing another look at Pauline, noticing the differences between them. Pauline uses her breasts to distract the men around her, and it works. Tru pretends she doesn't have breasts. Pauline leans into my father, watching him speak like he's the most fascinating man she's ever spoken to, touching him lightly on his wrist. Tru can't get within a foot of me without tensing up and looking like a rabbit ready to bolt.

Pauline probably has moves that are illegal in some states. Tru...well, for some damn reason she's the one that makes my jeans get tight just because she walked into the room.

And I'm worried about whatever trainwreck is about to happen but can't stop because Pops notices Tru finally and tells Pauline, "There she is."

My dad waves her over, and Tru stands next to me behind the bar. Pauline goes a little pale underneath her makeup, and she holds out her hand to Tru, but the bangles on her wrist tremble in a way she can't cover. "Hi, Tru. I'm Pauline."

Tru inhales a sharp breath and loses all the color in her face, too. My dad stiffens, finding his loyalty resides with the woman trying to steal the bar out from under his son and not the sex on legs sitting next to him. "You okay, honey?" he asks Tru.

My arm curves around her waist for support as she stares at Pauline's hand. "Why are you here?" she asks.

Pauline bites her lip and slumps as she withdraws her hand. "I didn't mean to startle you. I didn't think calling was the right thing to do. But I shouldn't have just shown up, either."

Dad and I exchange confused glances. "Everything all right, Yeats?" I ask, gently squeezing her hip.

She nods but I know she's not really okay because she hasn't reacted to the fact that I'm touching her. To Pauline, she stammers, "I'm so, so sorry," her eyes getting watery in a way that makes me want to heft her over my shoulder and carry her out of this bar. "I didn't know. You have to believe me. I didn't *know*."

"Oh, honey." Pauline's maneater facade goes away like a puff of smoke and a maternal, soothing voice replaces her purr. "I know you didn't. Richard was scum, pure and simple."

Holy shit. Is she Richard's other wife?

I look again at the two women and comparison doesn't work. Richard didn't have a type unless Pauline is rich too. Or was.

Tru still looks a little sick. "Maybe we should..." she looks around the near empty bar... "go sit down."

I squeeze her hip again. "Are you sure you're all right, Gertrude?"

"Yes, of course."

But I don't think she is. I think she's holding on for dear life.

"Look," Pauline says, not looking nearly as at ease as she did when she came in. "I'm not here to cause trouble. I just wanted to give you some money."

"What?" Tru and I ask at the same time. Tru finishes with, "I don't understand."

"He was a louse, but he sent me money for our son. It's not mine. You should have it. It belongs to you."

The breath seems to stutter in Tru's throat as she inhales. "You have a son?"

Pauline's face lights up. "Yeah. He's great. Did you and Richard..."

Tru shakes her head firmly. "No. No children."

My heart tumbles around my chest. Damn it. She wanted kids with the rat. I can't decide it it's unfair he never gave her any, or a blessing. I feel her pain, though, and it's a special kind of torture that there's nothing I can do about it.

My dad watches Pauline the whole walk to the table in the corner. Then he turns his head and grins at me.

Dirty old man.

They've been over there about ten minutes when Pops reaches over and smacks my shoulder.

"Hey. What was that for?"

"You're watching her like she's under surveillance."

"At least I'm not leering at her."

"I was talking about *Tru*."

I try not to rise to the bait. "I'm not watching Tru."

My dad huffs. "You're worried about her."

I shake my head. "In case you've forgotten, my livelihood is wrapped up in whatever is going on over there."

I wish Stella was here, not something I wish very often. Stella needs to get her own life so she stops insinuating herself into everyone else's, but she has a big heart. And huge ears. If she were here right now, she'd be able to listen in and report back. Who am I kidding? Stella would have invited herself to their table and just asked what she wanted to know.

My dad jars me out of my plot to infiltrate the enemy camp when he says, "That's not why you're watching her. You like her."

I slide him a look. "Dad, stop."

"She's a nice girl."

"She's uptight and annoying and she's trying to steal my business out from under me."

"You like her."

"I'm busy. Maybe you should go home."

"Son, I'm the only one in here. You're never busy."

When Pauline leaves, walked to her car by my father, Tru tries to tell me everything went fine. But she's quiet, more withdrawn than usual. She's not fooling me, so when we close the bar, I convince her to come with me for a walk with Fifi.

She's too quiet, but the night is still and pleasant, and finally she breaks her silence. "I really like her. Pauline."

I didn't expect that. Wouldn't most women hate the other woman, even if they were technically also the other woman? "She seems...nice."

"God, no wonder Richard...it doesn't matter. Obviously, Pauline is more his type than I was. She's probably every man's type. I almost feel sorry for him that he was stuck with me."

I would like to strangle Richard.

"Richard is a flea." Which was the only appropriate F-word that came to mind when I started speaking. In reality, Richard is a dumb fuck who better hope he never meets me. "Don't feel sorry for him that he had you and abused your trust. He didn't deserve you. He's an asshole."

"Well, Pauline didn't know about his other life either. He traveled a lot. They have a son. I can't take money from a single mom."

"It's your money, Tru."

"Is it? I don't know. If we were legally married and he had a son from a previous relationship, he'd have to pay support."

"With his money, Tru. His money. Not yours."

"Anyway, I like her. She was a stripper. That's how she met Richard. He went there a lot. To the club where she worked. He was a regular."

Strangling Richard might be too fast. I think a long, painful death is more what he deserves. It doesn't take a genius to know that the reason Tru thinks she's not sexual is because he made her feel that way. All the while, he was frequenting strip joints.

"How did she find you? How do you know she wasn't his partner and is still working the con."

"I don't have anything left for anyone to con me out of." She shivers so I take my coat off and wrap it around her shoulders. "She lives in Port Jacks. Not too far away, really. She got copies of all the bankruptcy papers. She figured she'd start here as Ironwing was the only thing not encumbered. Which is basically the same thing I did."

"Maybe she should take up being a private detective." I'm not sure I trust this Pauline, and I can't believe Tru does either. You'd think she'd be more careful.

We stop at the gazebo in the park and sit on the porch swing. "Anyway, when we sell Ironwing, I'll have enough money for what I need."

My back teeth are grinding against each other before she finishes her last sentence. It always comes back to that, doesn't it? Getting rid of Ironwing. "Sure."

"I'm selling my share—either to you or someone else. You know that, right?"

For some reason, I'm not really as worried about it as I should be. I should be talking to my lawyer. I should be trying to buy Tru out now. I should be doing a host of things that don't include sitting on a porch swing in the park with the closest thing I've ever had to an enemy.

If you don't include my mother.

Tru

I ROLL OVER AND WATCH the digital clock as the numbers change. There's no reason to get up early. The bar is closed on Sunday because Nash likes to have Sundays off.

I hardly slept last night, thinking about Pauline. How she should hate me, but she doesn't. I guess I should hate her too, but I don't. She's another victim of Richard, but she doesn't act like it. She's got confidence bigger than her boobs, and that's saying something.

It's hard to believe we shared a husband. Everything about the way she carries herself, the way she presents herself, how she says what she's thinking...just all of it is so anti-me. She oozes that feminine sexuality that is an actual foreign language if you ask my body. She uses it to her advantage, too, even to support herself once upon a time. She thought I would think less of her that she was a stripper when Richard met her, but part of me is jealous. Not the part that understands objectifying women is often misogynistic. But the paradox of using your body to get what you want. Mostly, just not being afraid of yourself, I guess, is what I'm jealous of.

I can't stay in this bed another minute.

Nash finds me in the kitchen still wearing pajamas holding a cookbook in one hand and a frying pan in the other. Without a word, he opens the cabinet and pulls out the fire extinguisher.

I set the book down. "Aren't you the funny one? See if you get any waffles."

"Waffles, huh?" He gives me a look, brows up. Infuriating. Hot. "How are you going to make waffles without a waffle maker?"

"How am I going to...Oh. I didn't...I didn't know." I try to hide the defeat in my voice, but really? Can I not make a fool out of myself for one day? I'd been wondering how I was going to make the little squares in the dough.

I used to think I was intelligent. Then I tried to live in the world. The real one, not the removed-from-reality penthouse where I didn't even get my own mail from a box.

Nash studies me; I look away. I don't have much dignity anymore, but I'd rather not see myself through his eyes. He slowly sweeps his fingers up my arm, over my throat, and then gently cups my jaw, turning it back to him. My breath hitches and my heart squeezes when he forces me to catch his gaze. "No shame in not knowing something."

The simple touch undoes me. That's new also. I knew the love of my parents briefly and my grandparents longer—but as kind and caring as they were, they were not demonstrative. Richard, well, we only made love a few times, and aside from that, occasional kisses to my cheek as he left for his travels was all I got.

My skin is still electrified from where Nash grazed me so lightly. Like it's waking up. Am I really so starved for human touch? It's probably a good thing Richard and I had no kids. Would I even know how to love them?

Nash teaches me how to make scrambled eggs. He doesn't say anything about the bits of shell in them while we eat at the kitchen counter.

"What are your plans for the day?" he asks, after swallowing the last of his coffee.

"I don't have any. Maybe Fifi and I will explore Brazen Bay some more."

"Alone?"

I shrug. "I'm used to exploring cities alone. I used to go to the museums and galleries in New York by myself."

"I thought all socialites traveled in packs."

"I didn't really fit in with the social groups. At any age."

He's waiting for more. In that quiet way he has, I can feel him pulling at the things I don't want to talk about. How pathetic I am, for starters. But he's quiet and watchful and I find myself telling him about my grandparents, their deaths. Richard. How it was difficult to maintain peer relationships when I was in school. How even as a married woman, I was alone most of the time. "After we got married, he wasn't around very often."

Not even holidays, though at least now I know why. He was with Pauline and Daniel, their son.

"Did you love him?"

"No."

"I see." He gets distant but pretends he isn't as he picks up our plates and takes them to the dishwasher.

"It wasn't like that. He didn't love me either. We were friends. I knew what I was getting into. At least, I thought I did."

"You married a man you didn't love."

"He offered me..."

His frown, the dark slash of his eyebrows, seems so strange on a face that doesn't fluster often that I don't finish my sentence. I just blink at him.

"What? What could he offer you that was worth that?"

"Why are you so angry about this?"

"I'm not angry," he says in a perfectly controlled, perfectly angry voice, then lets out a breath of male frustration. "I'm not angry."

Well, he's something. I feel it coming off him in waves. "You're disappointed in me."

"I don't have any right to that feeling either. Look, it's none of my business." His movements are choppy, not his usual laidback almost lazy way.

I don't know why I care so much what he thinks of me. I'm not even that same girl anymore. But it hurts. "He was kind to me."

Nash stops wiping the counter, his back to me, and his head hangs slightly.

I go on speaking to his back. "Richard was my friend. I thought. We never pretended to love each other. We just didn't want to live life alone. I thought." My hands start shaking, the remembered ache of loneliness so visceral. "I didn't want to be alone, Nash. I know you don't understand that because you've never been alone a day in your life. He offered me my only chance at a family, so I took it."

Nash turns slowly. "Your only chance? Why would you think he was your only chance?"

My heart hiccups at the look of him, the stillness of his expression. "Please don't make me say it." Not when he looks so virile and delicious, and I'm just a lump shaped like a woman who's never really felt like one.

"This is about you thinking you're not sexual again, isn't it?"

I try to slide past him, but he tugs me close.

"The last thing I want right now is for you to try to make me feel better. There's nothing wrong with me. Just because I'm not interested in—"

He places two fingers over my mouth. "Do not tell me you are not interested in sex. You're a lot of things, but a liar isn't one of them." He takes his hand off my mouth. "There's nothing wrong with you.

You're low on self-esteem and confidence, I'll give you that. But you are a warm-blooded, beautiful woman who could seduce any man you put your mind to. I know because I'm one of them."

"Nash..." I breathe, surprised, trembling, fluttering where I always seem to flutter if I think about him too much. I close my eyes when his hand cups my face and he bends low, covering my mouth with his.

I'm frozen in shock at first, the tender touch so surprising. So warm and wonderful. I can't resist for long and respond, coming alive like Sleeping Beauty after her long nap.

A husky groan leaves him and he changes the angle, deepening the kiss. Heat like I've never felt explodes inside me. This is what a kiss feels like when a man *wants* to do it.

When *I* want to do it.

He presses my mouth harder, and I open to him, allowing his tongue to sweep into my mouth and intoxicate me much faster than trying to get drunk ever has. His mouth is clever, gliding and nibbling, pushing and retreating. I clutch his solid, firm biceps and arch into him. I want to get a better taste of him. I want to feel him in the places where he's not touching me.

The riptide kiss pulls me far away from the safe shore I'm so used to, and all I can do is hold on to him.

He slows the kiss down, bringing it back to its tender beginnings. My rubbery legs are somehow still holding me up when he takes a step back. "It doesn't seem gentlemanly to tell you I told you so, so I'll infer it."

I narrow my eyes at him, but he just smirks. "That's the same thing."

He presses a different kind of kiss to the top of my head. "Richard the Flea was a dud in bed if you kiss like that but think you aren't interested in sex. But don't take my word for it. By all means, let me show you sometime."

"Nash..."

He winks at me. God, I love hating him. "Pops is making barbecue tonight. He prides himself on his sauce. I know he'd like it if you came by. You can ride with me if you want."

I nod, saved from saying something awkward when Fifi goes to the door.

Later that day, we're sitting on Brandon's deck overlooking the water. The salty air is nothing compared to the salty language between Nash and his dad, but their stories are funny, and I enjoy the good-natured teasing between them. Nash hasn't touched me since this morning, and luckily he hasn't mentioned the kiss. The kiss I can't stop thinking about.

Some kind of door has opened. Maybe more like the lid on Pandora's box. But I look inside at my frigid sexuality and now I have questions. Questions I think Nash could answer for me. But I'm also so afraid of letting my guard down, I don't know if I could let him.

Brandon brings out his guitar and sits next to me on a bench. Nash rolls his eyes at him. "That thing doesn't work on all the women you know. Have some self-respect."

Brandon ignores him, tuning the strings. "You play any instruments, Tru?"

"I played the violin poorly through middle school." I think of the beautiful piano that used to belong to my grandmother. "My grandmother played piano. She was quite good. And my grandfather used to play records but no instruments." Brandon laughs and forces the guitar at me. "No, I couldn't."

"Sure you can." He teaches me some chords, which I play poorly, but Brandon is as patient a teacher as his son. It takes me a minute to realize what I'm feeling. Peace. A sense of well-being. I'm not guarded. I'm not trying to politely engage someone's attention—they just give it to me here.

I look up and catch Nash watching me. I can't read the expression on his face, but it feels colder than what I hoped for.

Chapter Six

Nash

The ride home from my dad's house was awkward, and that was all my fault. There was a moment when she was laughing and playing the guitar, that she was so beautiful, she stole my breath. I had to remind myself that she's trouble. That she's upending my life.

That she could fit so *easily* into it.

Not that either of us want her to. Hell, I have never wanted to settle down. I like my life just the way it is. No drama.

So, I got spooked and cut the evening off early. Because inside, I'm twelve and don't know how to deal with complicated feelings. Damn it. Now I need to apologize.

I turn off the shower and wonder what the hell is wrong with me. It's not normal for me to sulk. She's done something to me. Some kind of spell, maybe. I bet if we just had sex, got it out of our systems, all this would turn around. It sounds dumb, even to me, but that kiss today...that was unlike any kiss I've ever had.

Get it together, McKendrick. It was just a kiss. The two of you have chemistry. Serious chemistry, but that's all it is. It's been brewing for a while, like something in a cauldron she cooked up, so of course it was going to boil over.

I nearly run her over as I'm coming out of the bathroom. I start to apologize until I see the look in her eye. She's dumbstruck.

Of me in a towel.

Who's cooking up the spell now, Gertrude?

She can't find words, she's just blinking, her mouth open, her eyes dilated. It makes me hot. And hungry.

"Are you ogling me, Dickinson?"

She blushes such a pretty color. "No. Yes. Not...I'm sorry."

"You don't need to apologize. I like being ogled." I waggle my brows, lightening the mood. Maybe we really should have sex. It doesn't seem like such a dumb idea now, looking at the naked desire in her eyes over my near naked body. She wants me. I want her. We're adults.

And I fucking love making her blush.

"Wanna dry my back?"

Her hands go to her hips, signaling that her mind is reengaged and she's about to get prissy again. "You know, you always drop these ridiculous innuendos on me because you know I get flustered. What if one time, I took you up on it?"

My cock twitches. "I'd be happy if you took me up on it." Every cell in my body would *rejoice* if she took me up on it. This would be the best way to stop those weird angsty feelings I keep getting around her. It's genius. I've never had problems detaching feelings from sex. It's always been one and done for me and the woman I'm with. By mutual consent. Tru should be no different. "Say the word and this body is all yours for the night."

Her upper lip curls, but I'm not buying her disgust. Her nips are clearly poking the pajama shirt she's wearing. "I think you just say things to make me blush."

"I really do like the way you blush. It makes me wonder how far down your creamy skin that shade of pink goes." I reach for her hand, pick it up, and kiss it. "Tell me what you want, Tru."

Please say me.

She's trembling. I like it, but not if it means she's scared. "I'm not the kind of woman you're used to. I don't really...enjoy the act."

"The *act*? C'mon, Tru. Did you ever think that maybe the reason you didn't enjoy 'the act' is because Richard wasn't any good at it?"

She ponders this. I can tell because you can practically see gears moving when she's thinking hard. "Are you saying that because of some sort of male one-upmanship contest to feed your ego, or do you really think he wasn't good at it?"

"Did he make you come?" She blushes and stammers nonsense in response. "Then he wasn't any good at it. Trust me."

She glances down, her eyebrows raise and her eyes widen as she sees the aroused state of her tits, and she crosses her arms over them. "And you think if I do the act with you, I will reach orgasm."

"I think if we fuck, you're going to forget your own name. Several times. Yes, you will come. Hard and often." In many positions. "You might even require hospitalization from coming so many times."

"You're being so lewd. I don't know how to respond to that. Nobody has ever talked to me or around me the way you do." I'm going to assume she doesn't know that the way she is biting her lip is a turn-on. At this point, she could probably cross her eyes and I'd think it was sexy.

But she doesn't understand that. Not yet. Richard really did a number on her. Whatever happens or doesn't happen with our bar, when she leaves this town, I intend to make sure she goes no longer doubting herself. I step further into her space, but give her room to back up if she wants. Instead, she traces a bead of water with her eyes as it travels to my collarbone. "Baby, sex is supposed to be lewd."

"I can't think when you use that voice," she says in a voice so soft it could be a whisper.

Perfect. I lower it even more. "Sex is supposed to be dirty and messy and uncivilized. That's part of what makes it great."

"What else makes it great?"

"Coming hard and often." She's intrigued. I can tell. "You're not going to let him win, are you?"

She inhales sharply. "What?"

"Didn't that flea take enough from you? He played you, yes. But are you going to let him keep doing it? Show him he didn't win. Use me for my body and show him."

"Use you." Her eyes narrow. "This is a dare? Do you honestly think you can dare me into your bed?"

"Yes, I honestly do."

Her chin goes down and she stares at her feet. "He told me that I was frigid. That it was all right with him. That it didn't matter. That sex wasn't the most important thing in a relationship," she confesses.

Jesus Christ. "I want five minutes alone with the guy. I swear to God, just five minutes." I take a deep breath. This stopped being a game the minute she said frigid. "Do you believe him?"

"I did," she answers, her voice mousier than I've ever heard it.

"Do you still?"

"I don't know."

"That's a lie. But we can work with it. If you don't know, what do you think the best way to find out is?"

"You think your penis has some kind of magical powers, and I'm just going to instantly thaw from its majestic abilities?"

"You can tell me how magical I am when we're through."

She rolls her eyes.

"And while I think you'll find my penis spectacular, maybe even majestic, I don't think you should count my hands and mouth out of the deal."

Now she's looking anywhere but at me.

"You're not frigid. I promise."

"It wouldn't mean anything. If we do this. It won't make me change my mind about the bar, so if you think you're going to seduce and con me—"

"Don't. Compare. Me. To. Him."

"Fine." She throws her arms open wide. "Seduce me," she says with all the enthusiasm of someone who just wants to stop arguing. She's not convinced, but I've got all night.

"You really don't think this is going to work, do you? You don't think I can make you come?" I step toward her again since she didn't bolt before, backing her into the wall. I kiss her neck, my mouth hot and teasing, and she closes her eyes. "I should tell you something first," I say, inhaling that tender spot behind her neck.

"Tell me what?" She's trying to sound reserved, so cool. There's nothing frigid about this woman. She just doesn't believe it yet.

"I have a favorite sex act. It's almost a fetish." She stiffens, either my words or the way I nibble her earlobe has caught her off guard. "Do you want to hear what it is?"

"No," she whispers.

"I think you do. I think you want to know that what I love more than anything is going down on a woman. I can do it for hours. I love eating pussy, Tru. I'm going to love eating your pussy."

I pull back and watch her face. She still looks shy and timid, looking up at me with wide eyes as my dirty words sink in to her thoughts and my big hands pull loose the row of buttons of her pajama shirt. I part the fabric and drag my fingers across her smooth skin, her soft rounded stomach. So sweet. Hooking my hands in the waistband of her pants and panties at the same time, I pull them down.

"Step out." She does as she's told, her eyes on my face.

"Yeah...that's it, pretty girl." I trace a finger between her generous breasts, the towel riding precariously low on my waist as I get harder and harder. I catch her gaze, wondering what she's thinking when my hand moves lower, circling the hollow of her navel. She sucks in a quick breath and nibbles her bottom lip.

I trace a slow finger back up and around each of her rosy, dusky nipples slowly, so slowly. The hard little points could cut glass. "You're so beautiful. Perfect."

"I can't believe this is happening."

"Believe it, Gertrude." That lightens the mood until I slide my hand down, rubbing gently at her slippery cleft. Her eyes look where I'm touching her, watching me stroke her most private place. "You're so wet for me already." I cup her chin in my other hand and lean down. I kiss her warm mouth, groaning when she opens immediately this time. I stroke her candy-sweet tongue against mine, kissing deeper, harder. She's delicious. "I'm going to make you come on my hand now."

I start with a slow, gentle rub, circling around her clit, adding pressure until her breathing changes. An urgent ache takes root deep in my belly, but this is for Tru. My own needs are going to have to wait. "That feel good?"

"It feels fine."

"Fine, really?" Her eyes are glassy, her heated pussy swollen and soaking my fingers, and she says *fine*. I whisper near the hollow of her ear, "Liar."

I keep my hand in her pussy, still slow and gentle, but I give in to the temptation of these tits, using my tongue until I can't stand it anymore and take a long, hot pull of one, sucking and moaning around it until she groans and trembles. She's fucking close. Frigid must mean something different to Richard than it does to me. I've barely gotten started and she's on the edge.

"I feel..."

"What, sweetheart? What do you feel?"

"So hot, so lightheaded...so needy. I need...oh." She makes the most erotic sound I've ever heard in my life and her hips start pumping against my hand.

"That's it, pretty girl. Let it go. Let it all go."

She's beautiful as she comes. The look of surprise mixing with hazy pleasure. I let her come back to earth before I slide down to my knees and kneel between her legs, ready to worship her like the goddess she is right now. I want inside her, more than I've ever wanted anything my whole life. But I make a promise, in a dark, husky voice I barely recognize as my own. "You're going to come on my tongue next." She squirms a bit. "Don't be shy now." I give her one long, slow lick. "You taste so sweet."

"I do?"

The note of disbelief in her quiet voice pisses me off. "Don't tell me he never...never mind. Of course he didn't. You are delicious." I press my tongue inside her until she's squirming with a different purpose this time. To get more of my mouth on her. "Mmmm." I moan into that honey-sweet pussy. Richard's loss is my gain.

I pull my mouth away and her hips rock toward me like she didn't mean them to. "Easy now. I just want to look at you." I use my thumbs to spread that pink, swollen flesh. "So pretty." That clit calls me and I suck at it, long and deep. The taste of her jolts all my senses and ignites a devouring hunger I've never felt before. I want to gorge on her. The blood is pounding in my ears, and I rub my face all around her mound, her inner thighs, wanting to drown in her juices. Coat myself in them.

She cries out my name and it spurs me into overdrive. I'm desperate for more—more of her scent, more of her taste, more of her feminine moans. I hike one of her legs over my shoulder, and she lets out a surprised gasp when I bury my face inside her. I alternate swirling my tongue over her clit and fucking her with it as deep as I can go. I can't get enough of her. My hungry rhythm soon has us both moaning. She buries her fingers in my hair until I feel her let loose, feeling the waves of her pleasure as she bucks hard into my mouth. I lick her through the orgasm, her sweet, creamy juices trickling down over my chin.

I want more, but her legs are trembling, and I need to get her onto my bed. I French kiss her pussy again, slowing as she pants hotly and quakes in full-body tremors. When I stand, her expression is dazed, not yet back from her trip.

I scoop her up, the towel finally losing its battle and rolling off my body as I stalk into my bedroom.

"Nash?"

"I'm going to fuck you now."

"Oh." She blinks rapidly.

"Is that okay?"

"Am I going to enjoy it as much as what you just did?"

"You're going to write sonnets about my dick, Gertrude."

"Well, then let's keep going."

She feels so good in my arms. I don't think I've ever carried a naked woman anywhere before and it's amazing. Like being a caveman.

And being a caveman comes with some other feelings I've never experienced before. The fact that I want to mark her and claim her as mine is new.

Tru

THE TRIP FROM THE WALL to the bed is a blur. He throws me onto his mattress, but his hand behind my head protects me from hitting. There aren't any more teasing words, this man is different from the one who goads me into getting flustered. I haven't even had a chance to see him without the towel, but he doesn't slow for me to peruse his now naked body. With singular intensity, he lowers his head and sucks at my center again, hard and vicious, his fingers dancing inside me, stroking. I'm overcome with new emotions that I don't understand. Dark ones. Feral ones. His fingers pump me, and I gasp, urging him on. I reach for my own breast and squeeze as his slippery lips almost pinch at my clit. When he sees me touching myself, his eyes go even darker.

He works my flesh harder now, pulling and pushing, nipping and stroking. He's so rough, earthy, so unlike the civilized experiences I've had in the past. I never thought I would like it, but I do. I love it. I need it. One nip is more a bite and I squeal in pleasure, knowing it will leave a mark on my thigh. I squeeze my breasts harder and he growls, lavishing more delicious abuse, snarling like an animal, holding my hips tight until he's had his fill.

I lose track of the world as a powerful orgasm sweeps through me, but he doesn't let up. I'm helpless in his grasp, shaking and crying as sparks of pleasure so intense they border on pain ravage my quaking limbs.

He climbs up my body, his smile predatory as he rolls a condom onto his rigid cock and settles himself between my spread legs. "Such a messy girl. So wet." He grips my leg and nudges part of his cock-head into me, easing his weight over me deliciously, squeezing me apart as he pushes in.

I tense. He's so much bigger than what I'm used to.

"Easy, honey." The deep tone of his voice soothes me, relaxing my body, and he pushes in a bit harder, working himself slowly into me. "So tight. So wet for me."

I'm full of him, almost uncomfortably so. With the fullness comes another ache, a wanting, a feeling that this is something I am meant for. Taking this man into my body. He grasps my forearms and pins them down with his full weight. I really am helpless now. Thrillingly so. I close my eyes and moan.

He rocks gently, swaying inside me, until I start to rock my hips with him, finding a rhythm. Joining him where I once would lie still and let it happen. When I open my eyes, he moans as if the eye contact is an erotic shock. "You drive me wild, Tru. It's like you're inside of me even though I'm the one inside of you."

I'm not prepared for him to say such a thing. It's like a confession, an intimacy that goes beyond what our bodies are doing. Nash starts a steady, shallow slide, and the pleasure grows hotter and hotter inside me. I surely can't orgasm again, can I? I wrap my legs around him, my heels digging into his body for leverage.

"Yeah, that's it. Fuck me back, honey. Work my cock. You make me feel like a fucking beast." His head dips and his breath falls across my chest in bellows. We're reaching for something bigger than we are, the building of ecstasy surging through both of us.

He presses his forehead against mine, falling back to a slow, gentle rhythm, not wanting to rush us even though I feel like I'll die if I don't come again. We look at each other for a long moment, breathing through the awareness. Capturing this moment.

"Nash, I love the way you feel inside me. I can feel you everywhere."

He mutters something, sitting up on his knees and taking hold of my legs without slipping out. Slowly, smoothly, he pushes deeper inside me, deeper than I thought he could go. He's holding my legs open obscenely and giving me long, slow strokes, over and over, pushing into me. "Your pussy is grabbing my cock. You must like this. Does your tight, little pussy like my cock, Tru? Watch me fuck you, honey."

His cock, thick and wet, slides out from between my legs between the dark mess of my pubic hair. I can't believe it's me, so lewd and sloppy and wanting more. He pushes back in, vanishing into my dark curls.

The pleasure coils inside me, and I can't stop the frantic bucking of my hips, the loud moans bellowing out of me. My legs lock behind him, working him into my body as far as he can go. He's smiling down at me like the devil. Amused by me, by the things he's making me feel. Fine. That's fine. I like feeling this way. I want to push him just as far as I can. I pull his head down and whisper, "Fuck me." Wiggling my hips and trying to use my inner muscles to squeeze him, I groan and say louder, "Please, fuck me, fuck me..."

Nash grabs my shoulders from underneath and bangs into me hard and fast like a man possessed, like my words pushed him over the edge. "Beg me some more, honey."

"Please make me come, Nash. I need it. I need you. I need you to fuck me with that huge cock until I come."

The pure masculine growl fills the room as he fucks me so hard I can't breathe. The slap of our bodies, the sweat forming on our skin, the banging of the headboard on the wall—we're both taken over by this savage lust as his big body moves over mine. My orgasm washes over me in long, crushing waves but Nash doesn't stop moving. "Take me, take me, take all of me," he yells until he stiffens. I feel him swell even bigger somehow, and then his body convulses as his hands tighten on me, squeezing me too hard. I love it. He groans into my neck, nearly sobbing my name as he comes, and I hold him as tight as I can, wishing there was no condom, wishing I could be sticky and covered and filled with his cum.

He stays there on top of me, gasping, slowly pulling and pushing his cock in and out of me, wringing out every last drop of our pleasure. He murmurs my name and rolls us over, still inside me, so that my face is on his chest.

My body is trembling with aftershocks. I am deliciously bruised and will be so sore tomorrow. "I'm not really frigid, am I?" I ask into the dark when my heart slows and breath returns to my lungs.

"No, Gertrude. I'm certain of it."

I smile into his chest, lulled by his heartbeat. He takes care of the condom, brings me water, and slides into bed. I intend to go to my own room, but sleep steals my ambition.

When I wake up, it's to Nash rearranging my limbs and trying to sneak out of bed without waking me up.

Chapter Seven

Nash

The complicated maneuvers of getting out of bed without waking the other person up are completely new to me. I haven't woken up with someone in my bed before. I don't bring women to my bed. I only accept invitations to bed when my partner knows I'm not staying after.

It was a mistake to sleep with Tru. The sex was off the charts, but the post-cuddle should never have happened. She's in a vulnerable place, and she's going to equate orgasms with deeper meaning. If I'd have gently returned her to her own bed last night, she'd know where we stand, but no, I did everything exactly wrong and now I have to extricate myself from my own bed.

I manage to roll her over onto her own side in a move I'm ashamed to admit I learned from Chandler Bing. I'm moving as slowly and gently as I can when her voice stops me cold.

"Where are you going?"

I feel like I'm in the spotlight. Maybe not on stage, more like a police flashlight—caught red-handed. "Bathroom," I manage.

"Then why are you sneaking out of bed?"

She props her chin on her hand and studies me, not saying a word.

"I'm not sneaking. It's my house, my bed, and my bladder. If I want to go the bathroom, I don't need to run it by you first."

Her eyes widen in surprise and then she laughs. "You're a little touchy. Usually you're in a much better mood in the mornings." She stretches indulgently, the sheets riding low enough for me to catch the tops of her rosy breasts.

Morning wood just became a fucking Redwood tree.

"I know I'm in a much better mood this morning." Her sleepy eyes are heavily lidded and the smile on her face makes her look like a happy cat in the cream. Which makes me think of her creamy pussy, and how happy she made me last night. "I cannot believe I've been missing out on that for all these years. That was nothing like what I've experienced before."

My chest fills with male pride knowing how satisfied I made her. "I told you Richard was bad in bed."

What I don't say is that last night wasn't like anything I've ever experienced before, either. That I have a sneaking suspicion that it wasn't my performance that made it so great. I'd like to write it off on the delayed gratification of finally getting her into my bed after being attracted to her for weeks. Or the fact that I hadn't gotten laid in a while.

That makes sense. Once I get out of bed and get back into the normal rhythm of my day, it won't feel like something hit a fault line in my heart, ripping it open and exposing me to the elements.

Because we are not going there.

"Look, I have things to do. I'm not trying to be rude, which is why I didn't wake you. I just think it's best we get back to normal."

"Back to normal. Are you kidding? I am not ever going back to normal."

I can feel my face paling. Jesus, I'm such a coward. "Gertrude..."

"Wow, you are really freaked out, aren't you?" She sits up, clutching the sheet to her chest. "I'm talking about me, not you. I'm not going back to sub-zero temperatures now that I know what it's like on the other side. I intend to have a lot of sex from now on." She murmurs, "A lot. A lot. A lot."

In theory, that sounds amazing, but the compressed, tight ball of fear in my gut turns my mouth to dust. "Tru, I don't want you to get the wrong idea..."

"Would you relax?" She moves quickly, straddling me, and damn, she's damp and ready. "If you're not up for it, I'll find someone else." She wiggles against my erection. "But it feels to me like you're up for it."

Every caveman instinct I have comes roaring to the surface. Someone else? Does she think someone else can give her as much pleasure as I can? My eyes lift from those amazing tits to her face. Wait just a minute here. "That sounds like a dare. Do you think you can get me into bed on a dare?"

"As a matter of fact," she slides that warm pussy along my aching cock, wetting it with juices, but not letting me inside. "I do. You should probably teach me a lesson."

I stop her glide, grab a condom, and pull her over the tip of my aching cock when it's ready. She arches her back and slowly slides down the length of me, her neck elongated, her eyes closed as she concentrates on the feeling of ecstasy. She's beautiful, luminous. And I forget everything but watching her learn to ride.

TWO HOURS LATER, I call in a favor from Stella, of which I have more than a few owed me, and she covers me at the bar for the rest of the day. I stay away from Ironwing, from the apartment, and from my sexy roommate all day and well into the night. When I creep into the house, she's asleep in her own bed and Fifi growls at me.

"Keep your opinions to yourself, little gerbil."

She's still staring at me with judgment clouding her gaze. I've become used to the *adoration* clouding her gaze, and this new look sort of bothers me.

"What do you know? You're a dog."

She whines and puts her chin on her paws.

"It's for the best that we nip this in the bud. Trust me, it's best for you too. You don't want your mistress getting attached to me and then having her heart broken. I'm not interested in a relationship. It's better for all three of us this way."

I even give the ungrateful rat an extra treat before I go to bed, alone, and try not to think about the way it felt to wake up wrapped around a warm woman. To smell her hair and hold her sleeping, relaxed body against mine.

At the bar Tuesday night, she's acting like nothing is wrong. Which is what I want, but it pisses me off. Leo and Dixie are teaching her how to play darts, and every time I look over there, she's smiling and laughing and it makes me want to throw something, preferably the dartboard. Right through the window and onto the street.

I catch sight of something on the wall near the board that I hadn't seen before. I stalk over to it, grateful for something tangible to be upset at. "How long has this been here?" I demand, pointing my finger at the new mirror like a man finding a lover in his wife's bed.

She takes a dainty sip of her tea. Because now we serve tea in a damned bar. "It came in yesterday. Isn't it great? I found a bunch of retro beer mirrors on eBay, but this is the only one I found with an Ironwing logo." She traces her finger over the band logo and smiles softly.

It probably is really great, but all I see are spots. "Stop making changes without discussing it with me first. I don't want you redecorating the bar. Next you'll have lace curtains on the windows."

Her head tilts and she eyes me curiously, setting down her tea on a coaster. "Where is this coming from? Why are you so mad at me about a mirror? I didn't even use the business account."

"I'm not mad," I say through clenched teeth.

Her gray eyes ice over and she clasps her hands, linking her fingers together in front of herself, drawing inward. "All right," she agrees with me warily. I'm such an asshole, but I don't know how to stop this roll now that I've gotten going. Gone is the smiling, laughing woman playing darts with friends. *My* friends. Returned is the out-of-place woman from weeks ago. That's my fault too. "I can close the pub if you like." Her tone is cool, controlled. Chilled really. "Maybe you could go put your feet up or watch television upstairs. What is it that Stella says? Take a Midol."

"Are you coddling me?" I snarl, my mood slapping us both. "I said I'm not mad."

She holds her hands up in surrender. "Fine. *You* close then. I'm going upstairs to put *my* feet up." She calls Fifi to her.

"Leave her. She needs to go for a walk. I'll take her when I lock up."

Tru scoops the dog up. Her eyes are glittering, but she's honed her Park Avenue persona well, lifting a haughty chin in my direction. "I believe I can manage walking my own dog."

I can't tell her that I don't want her outside in the dark by herself. But, shit, I don't want her outside in the dark by herself.

She leaves, not giving me the satisfaction of a backward glance, and Leo and Dixie are staring at me like they're embarrassed they witnessed our fight. "It's nothing," I tell them.

They look at each other, the kind of couple that can communicate without using words. "We should get going."

"You can stay. Finish your game."

"I think we'll just go."

I think I am fucked.

Why did I start an argument with her? I look at the offending bar mirror and shake my head. My dad is going to love it. The patrons will love it. If I had found it, I would love it. But no, I had to make her feel bad for no reason other than I don't want her to be comfortable here in my world when she has made me feel so out of place in it.

Tru

A WOMAN WALKS INTO a bar with a dog sounds like the beginning of a joke or a repeat of my not-so-distant past, but this time the woman is Stella and the dog is definitely not well-groomed or in a Louis Vuitton carrier.

He's some kind of terrier. Probably. Black and white and grizzled. His tongue lolls out and his eyes look a little deranged. But when she puts him on the floor, he and Fifi are instantly smitten with each other. Sniffing and tail wagging commence immediately.

"No," Nash says. Which is one word more than he's said to me this morning. He did manage a gruff "I'm sorry" last night. He didn't elaborate, so I'm not sure what he's sorry for. Getting upset about rock memorabilia? Being rude to me? Avoiding me since we had sex? Maybe he's sorry we had sex at all. That's probably likely.

Which is a shame. I'd like to test some more of my non-frigid boundaries, but apparently, he's taken it upon himself to decide that I can't handle the intricacies of a no-strings affair. He also doesn't realize that he's the one having a hard time with it, not me. I'm not interested in a relationship. I've learned my lesson about relying on a man and am not keen about getting put in that position again. Passion—that's different. I'd love to explore that some more. Eradicate the old me completely.

"Take that dog right back from wherever you got him from."

Stella pouts, then remembers it's Nash and pouting doesn't work on him. "Please, Nash. His name is Bo and he's a really nice boy. I had to go pick him up from death row at a shelter in the city today. He's meant to be yours."

"I don't want a dog." All three of us look at Fifi who finished sniffing Bo and is now sitting on Nash's foot proprietarily.

Stella ignores the obvious. "I did a reading last night and used the pendulum this morning. Bo is meant to be with you. The cards and the pendulum agree. Please."

Bo stretches the leash to sniff at Fifi, and Nash pulls her up off the floor protectively. "Back off, buddy."

"He won't hurt her. They were both wagging their tails. Put her down. You'll see."

It pains him, but he puts Fifi back down, letting the dogs get to know each other some more. "Fifi is only here temporarily. What will I do with a dog when they go?"

He almost spits the word *they* out.

Stella's gaze catches mine for confirmation and I nod. Stella bites her lip, thinking how to spin this now. "Could you at least take him until I find another home for him?"

"How stupid do you think I am, woman?"

"You don't really want me to answer that, do you?"

The mailman comes in with my package, thank you Prime, and it distracts Grumpy McGrumperson long enough for Stella to "have to run," leaving Nash with a new dog and a promise to call later.

He rounds on me. "I thought we agreed no purchases without discussing them first."

I take a deep breath, not understanding why he keeps trying to draw me into fights with him. "I'm sorry you're upset with Stella, but please don't take it out on me."

He pulls out a pocket knife and takes the box off the counter. "What is it this time?" he asks.

I try to snatch the package. "It's mine."

He's got it open before I can get it back, telling me all about how he likes the way the bar is now, it looks just fine, and I have no right to just come in and turn his life upside down and now he has two dogs...and then all the color leaves his face when he pulls out a long box with a purple penis on it.

He brings his eyes to mine and our gazes catch for a long moment when time slides into another reality briefly. He blinks once. Twice.

I cross my arms over my chest. "It's not for the bar. It's for my vagina. And if you'd be so good as to put it back in the box, I'd appreciate it."

"You bought a dildo?"

I snatch it from him and lower my voice so...well, there's no one in the bar to overhear, but I do it anyway. "Yes."

"Why?"

"You don't really want me to answer that, do you?" He just blinks at me some more. Waiting. "We've established that I'm not frigid. *You* don't seem to want to continue what we started, and you appeared jealous when I suggested that maybe I find another lover—"

"I don't get jealous," he interrupts, his jaw so tight I can hear his teeth grinding.

"Yes, all right. Anyway, I thought it best not to let the pipes freeze back up. Stella recommended this model to me...why are you recoiling in horror?"

"Stella has a purple...one of those?" He gestures to the box in my hand.

"Well, actually, I don't know what color hers is. I thought purple was kind of whimsical, so I—"

"Whimsical?"

"Why do you even care? You have made your position very clear. You are counting the days until I leave and you don't want me to insinuate myself into your life any more than I already have. I thought I was being very mature by not flaunting finding another paramour under your nose."

"What's a paramour?"

It's a very good thing I don't carry a small knife in my pocket the way he does. That's all I'm saying. "Do not make fun of the way I talk. You know very well what a paramour is. I'm going to go put this away upstairs and then I am going to meet Pauline for lunch. If we're done here, of course."

His tense jaw squares even more. "Yes, we are done here."

"Wonderful. Would you like me to take Fifi or leave her here to keep Bo occupied while I'm gone?"

He picks up a towel and a glass, his go-to activity when he's thinking. "Just leave her."

PAULINE TAKES A BITE out of her meatball grinder, though she's hanging on my every word. We've got the corner table, but I try to keep my voice down. This town has ears in the walls, I think.

"He's just trying to protect his heart. He's striking out at you," she explains, "hoping that you'll get mad and either break things off for good or say something he'll be able to pin all the blame on when things don't work out. It's classic."

"Well, that makes no sense at all."

"Did you think it was going to?"

I contemplate my potato chip, but the answer isn't there. "But there is nothing to work out. We aren't involved. There's nothing to break off between us."

"I wouldn't be so sure."

"Trust me. It was a fling."

Pauline nods. "Sure, it was."

"We have nothing in common. He resents my very presence. He doesn't like my dog or my ideas."

"Honey, he loves that damn dog. Have you looked at him with her? And if you could see the way he looks at you when you're not paying attention, you'd see what the rest of us do."

I sit back, unable to eat another bite, but knowing I'll somehow find the room to put the whole sandwich away before this lunch is over. "So you've only met him a handful of times. What are you basing this knowledge on?"

She blushes. Which I'm sure she doesn't do very often. "Brandon talks about him a lot."

"Brandon, huh?"

"I'm not sleeping with him, if that's what you're thinking," she quickly interjects, her features frozen in an almost stoic expression.

"Why not?" I cover her hand with my own. "Pauline, I wouldn't judge you if you were. You know that, right?"

A secret smile crosses over her features. "Sorry…I just…people are used to making rash judgments about me. But I'm not. We're friends. For now, we're friends."

"Do you have feelings for him? More than friend feelings?"

She lifts one shoulder. "I feel like I should take my time. I don't want to get burned again."

It feels really good to have a friend, a girl friend, to talk to about crushes and men. Nobody has ever filled this role for me before, and now I have Pauline and Stella. But I can't talk to Stella about Nash. Our talks are more general…what kind of sex toy is best, which wine goes with Sara Lee Cheesecake…that kind of thing.

But my ex-husband's wife? I feel like she's my sister somehow. Sister wives is the wrong vibe, but sister friends is pretty close.

"Brandon is a nice man." Despite raising such a dimwitted buffoon. That was unkind. Despite raising an *intelligent* buffoon. I can honestly say that Nash isn't dimwitted in the least, though he is content to let others believe he is simpler than he is.

"Brandon wants to take me on a real date. I keep putting him off."

"Why?"

"I have to think of Danny. I don't know…following my heart has led me to some trouble in my life. And I'm not always sure it's my heart I followed when all is said and done. My ovaries make horrible life decisions, so I'm trying to pay more attention to my brain, I guess."

"That makes sense. Except I can tell you that following your brain sometimes leads you astray too." My heart wasn't involved when I married Richard. For sure not my ovaries. I guess it wasn't my brain either. It was fear. Fear of being completely alone in a world where I was already so lonely.

We get quiet after that. "I think you should seduce him," she says as if we were still talking about Nash.

"I don't think that's a great idea. Why don't you seduce Brandon instead?

"I think with Brandon, it would be best if I let him work for it a little longer. Make sure this is what we both want. I think the problem with Nash is he's thinking too much. You both are. Seduce him."

I look at her, all made up, dressed to slay from her sexy hair to her red-clawed hands to the stiletto heels. "I think the world works a little differently for someone like me, Pauline. I don't have your skills at seduction."

"Well, you do dress like my grandma, but that hasn't stopped him from wanting you."

I throw my straw wrapper at her. "This coming from Peg Bundy."

She throws it back. "Underneath, you got the goods. Use that instead of your softer side of Sears getup."

Right. She's right.

Could I seduce Nash?

I bet if we have sex one more time, it will get him out of my system. We can end things on better terms. But my clothes and lingerie won't do it. My very boring lingerie. My even worse clothes.

My lingerie wouldn't seduce anyone. I'm going to have to be more creative.

That night, after closing, I race upstairs while he walks the dogs. I light candles, I hide the television remote, and I tear off my clothes.

When he comes in, I'm sitting on the couch wearing one of his shirts and reading a book.

One of his eyebrows shoots up when he looks at me. "What are you doing?"

I set the book on the table and look over the top of my reading glasses. "I'm testing a theory."

"What theory is that?"

"You said I can't learn life from books." His eyes narrow. "I want to try something I learned in a book." I glance at the book on the table and look back at him, waiting for him to notice the Kamasutra book's title.

Chapter Eight

Nash

The sight of her wearing one of my button-up shirts makes me want to beat my chest and swing from a vine. Her hair's up in a messy bun, her glasses are perched precariously on her nose, and she's blinking at me a little too innocently.

"What did you learn in a book?" I glance at the title, hoping it's not a cookbook. I have a high fire insurance deductible.

Holy shit. It's not a cookbook. She's reading erotic literature on my couch while half-dressed and one hundred percent sexy. Every available brain cell I have just died and all I can think of is the ways she tastes.

She rises to her knees and brings the book up to her chest. "It says here there are thirty kinds of kissing."

My ears start ringing and stars circle my vision like I'm in a damn cartoon.

"I don't think I've experienced thirty different kinds, though I bet you used several of these on me the other night. Maybe you're right. Maybe I can't learn everything from a book. Maybe some things just need to be experienced to be understood."

I don't think. I'm past the ability to do so anyway. I haul her to me and crush her mouth to mine. I don't know the number of this type of kiss, but it's full of frustration. Hunger. I'm furious with her, with myself.

She clings to me when she should push me away. My hands roam her back until they're under the hem of my shirt and I've got two handfuls of her luscious ass. I squeeze. "This is all a setup, isn't it? You're seducing me on purpose."

She pulls her head back far enough to answer. "Of course I am."

"Just wanted to be clear."

We tumble onto the couch and all I know is the way she tastes, her scent, her soft skin. I haven't had a make-out session on a couch in a really long time. I kiss her harder, my tongue dancing past her lips. Panting, I break the kiss and rest my forehead against hers. "I don't like how easy it is for you to manipulate me."

She looks up at me a little shyly but smiling. "Do you want me to stop?"

"Hell, no." I want her desperately. "I don't think you should just get away with it though."

"You're right. I've been such a naughty girl. You better teach me a lesson."

My hand grabs the back of her head, pulling her up. Tru gasps as my lips crush into hers again. I cup her firm, pert breast, squeezing and caressing under the material of my shirt.

Growling, I shift, pushing my body down against hers, pinning her to the couch as I kiss her. She purrs against my mouth and arches her back, pushing those sweet curves into me.

I'm lost.

I pull the shirt open, rending the buttons from the material. Like a striking snake, I dip my head and take a naked tit in my mouth, sucking hard on that little pink bud. She moans and writhes under me, and I press my fingers against the bare folds of her wet pussy.

Wait, bare. She wasn't bare last time.

Startled, I lean back.

"I tried another experiment," she says sheepishly.

I chuckle. "You're one surprise after another." She still has a tiny triangle of hair, almost an arrow in case I get lost. But there's no chance of that, not when my fingers slide so easily where I want to be most.

"Oh," she moans as my fingers work within her. I drop my head to suck on her luscious tits, licking and biting her hard nipples, drawing startled cries from her gasping mouth. It appears she likes it a little rough, which is all I need to spur me on.

I move all my attention lower, working two fingers in and out of her. She's tight. Warm, moist, slippery. So erotic. Her hips are moving in time with my fingers, encouraging my actions. She begins to make little moans of pleasure, so I continue working her up before turning my fingers over, face up, and begin my search for that hidden spot maybe she doesn't even know about yet.

There it is. I can feel the spongy patch, swollen with excitement. I use my middle finger to rub it softly, back and forth. She's got her breasts in her own hands, pushing them together and the cleavage creates a new item for my bucket list of places I want to put my dick.

Her scent is powerful and erotic, drugging all my senses. Her body pitches, shaking. "That's it, baby, I want you to come." I press harder on her clit with my thumb and she loses all control. A small amount of clear liquid shoots out of her and onto my hand as her body convulses around me.

When the final spasms of her orgasm pass, I sit up, my hungry eyes devouring every inch of her beautiful, naked body from her tangled hair, her flushed face, the soft curves of her tits, her rounded hips, her wet, swollen pussy.

I've never been so in awe of any damn thing in my life.

"What *was* that?" she asks, not so smug anymore.

"That was the hottest fucking thing I've ever seen in my life." I ease my hand out of her. "You're amazing."

"Should I be embarrassed? I feel like I..."

"You didn't pee yourself. You just rewarded me with a very rare and wonderful thing people sometimes call female ejaculation. But maybe we can discuss it in more detail later." I pull her hand to me, pressing her fingers against the hard bulge straining within my jeans. She sits up and opens my jeans, pulling out my hardened, thick shaft. It's soaked with precum.

Her fingers close around me and slowly stroke the length. "I didn't really get to see this the other night. We got rushed."

"We're going to get rushed again."

My mind starts working on the fastest way to get to a condom when her mouth opens and her lips slip quickly around the head of my dick. I throw my head back and groan in pleasure as her warm, wet mouth engulfs me. My pleasure starts building too fast, my hips rocking and thrusting involuntarily. "Not so fast, Tru."

I have to pull her off my dick, God bless her. I practically throw her down and settle myself between her legs. With a hard thrust, I bury myself to the hilt in her wetness. Her body spasming under me, she cries out as I thrust too vigorously into her.

"Did I hurt you?"

She scores my back with her fingernails. "No."

"Oh, fuck," I groan. "Fuck, you feel good. You like this cock inside you?"

"Yes."

I'm too rough, but she's clawing me right back, quivering and shaking under me as I drive into her over and over again.

Her pussy tightens around me, milking me as she shatters, and with one final thrust and a roar, my body tenses and unloads deep inside her, spasm after spasm. An alarm tries to go off in my head, a warning, but all I can do is collapse my shaking body on top of her.

For a long time we lay together, limbs tangled and sweaty.

And sticky. So damn sticky.

I have never come inside a woman without a glove. She's done something to me. Some kind of spell. She turns off my brain and turns on my inner caveman.

"I'm sorry, Tru. I didn't use a condom."

The sweaty spell is broken and she sits up, untangling from me. My shirt is hanging off just one of her wrists, the button holding it on her. Why is that hot?

"I'm on the pill. And after I found out I wasn't in a monogamous marriage, I had every test there is performed...twice." She shudders. "You?"

"I get tested regularly." I sit up all the way, bracing my elbows on my knees and holding my head in my hand. What a goddamned downer this kind of discussion can be after the hottest sex I've ever had. "I haven't been with anyone else recently."

She's trying to get the shirt back on, but it's all twisted around making her one hot, disheveled mess. "Define recently."

I exhale loudly. "It's been at least six months for me. And this is the only time without protection."

She nods then surprise colors her features. "Six months? I just assumed..."

"I'm a careful man, Gertrude. You should know that by now."

Things are strained between us when it feels like we should be closer than ever. It doesn't make sense to me. I'm not the guy who needs or wants a relationship with a woman. Sex has always been just sex, and I don't know why this is different. Why the intimacy seems more important, and the lack of it right now makes me hollow inside.

Maybe I'm changing. Maybe she's changing me. I go to bed, alone, because I need to think about this. Weigh it in my mind.

In the morning, I find her business plan on the desk in the office downstairs and realize she still plans to sell the bar.

What am I *doing*?

She breezes into the office, looking relaxed and well-sexed. A fist squeezes my heart when I realize how beautiful she is. How much I want her both naked and fully clothed in my office.

She loops her arms around my neck. "I'm wondering if I can still get a refund on my sex toy. I don't think I'm going to need it after all. Not after last night."

Fuck. I forgot all about that damn thing. I close my eyes against the flash fantasy of using it on her myself. I wonder if it has any special features. Does it vibrate? I'd love to torture her to the edge and back over and over again.

I sigh and pull her arms off my neck, pulling away from her before she can kiss me.

I need space, and I have none. She's in my apartment, in my bar, and in my head. Next stop is my heart if I'm not careful, and that business plan on the desk means my foolish heart needs to wake up and smell the coffee.

I learned from my mother that wanting more than you have is dangerous. That's how you get hurt. I promised myself I'd be content with what I have and never yearn for what I don't a long time ago. It's time to remember who I am.

Tru

I LOOK UP FEMALE EJACULATION in between pulling drafts, and am relieved I didn't wet myself last night, but I'm not sure how I feel about Nash knowing secrets about my body that I didn't even know.

He's acting weirder today than even yesterday. I thought we went someplace new, but now he's running even faster in the other direction.

After we close the pub, I turn on some jazz standards, but he doesn't spin me around the bar like before. I'm trying to work up some anger, but when I sneak looks at him, he's so...sad. His long face is pulling feelings from me like...*go comfort him.* But the wall he's built is awkward. I really don't know what to do. I thought I had it handled with the "just seduce him" thing, but that only seems to work in the moment. A very fine moment, but it doesn't carry over.

I don't even know what I want from him. I thought it was just the sex. But the space around my heart is physically aching from the space between us. I want the friend. I want the lover. I want the business partner. But it feels like I might only end up with "that guy I used to know."

What a sad thought. That space around my heart squeezes a little more.

I really like Nash. Most of the time. He's funny, level-headed, more caring than he knows. He's a good man. Despite my disturbing his whole life, he's shown me how to stand on my own feet. How to learn new things. He takes care of me without making me feel like I can't do it myself.

We make it through the whole day acting like strangers. This evening, he is hanging up the dog leashes on the hooks he installed near the apartment door this afternoon when he hangs his head.

"Nash, what is wrong? You've been acting strangely all day."

He crosses the room like it's the corridor to the electric chair. "I don't want you to get the wrong idea about us. What this is."

"Okay." My head is held high, but my knees feel a little shaky. He's breaking things off then.

"I'm not trying to hurt your feelings."

I nod. Of course not. "Have I done something wrong?"

He tunnels his hands through his thick hair, mussing it up sexily. "No, of course not. We just need to create better boundaries. We are done with the sex."

"I see." Shame fires inside my belly. "This is about the...squirting thing, isn't it?" I should have known it wasn't as great as he pretended.

"No. Not at all." His hands clench into fists, once, twice. "That was actually the most awesome thing ever. This has nothing to do with you. It's just...with us living together... I mean in the same apartment, and working together, the sex is confusing things. It's getting too domestic."

The old Tru is trying to break into my thoughts with embarrassment or low confidence, but the new Tru, the one I'm building from scratch, is actually doing some quick calculations.

He continues as if he can't see the shift coming over me. He goes into the kitchen and starts the kettle, pulling two mugs down and opening the box of tea. "I don't want you to get the wrong idea. I'm not the settling down type."

I cross my arms over my chest, watching him as he carries on with making tea. *Tea.* "You certainly are not domesticated at all."

He apparently doesn't hear the sarcasm. "Right. That's what I'm saying." He gets a fresh towel out from the drawer and wipes down the counter. "I like being single. And you're the kind of woman who needs a different kind of man."

"Sure I am."

He switches the magnet on the dishwasher and opens it to empty it, pulling out the rack. "Why is your dildo in here?"

"I wanted to clean it before I used it."

He stands up and scrubs his hands over his stubbled cheeks. "Right, okay. You haven't, uh, used it yet."

I shake my head and meander over. We both stare at it. "No. Haven't had a chance. Guess I will now. Since you and I are done with the whole sex thing."

He swallows hard, his hands clenching and unclenching repeatedly. "Tru...I—"

Whatever he was going to say is swallowed by the shrilling whistle of the kettle. He shakes his head to clear it and pulls the kettle off the heat, pouring the water into the cups.

But not in a domesticated way, of course.

"I'll just take my tea into my room," I say, making a show of plucking the dildo from the rack first. "Thank you for being honest with me."

I smile and he narrows his eyes. "You're thinking that you're going to seduce me again. You think I have no willpower and that the idea of you and that purple...that I won't be able to stop myself."

"Nope. I heard you loud and clear. We are done having sex together. You don't want me to fall for you because you are happy being alone, so you're doing me a big favor by saving my heart from the inevitable breakup that is coming because you don't think I can handle a purely sexual relationship."

"What are you up to?"

"I'm up to having a purely sexual relationship with my new toy. I hope I don't develop too many feelings for it. Since I'm prone to throwing my heart around, obviously."

"I knew you wouldn't take this well."

"I'm taking it just fine. I think what you want is for me to throw myself at your feet and beg you to love me, but that's not going to happen. I was just fine with having a lover. I'm happy being single. I think *you* are the one getting all the feels, as Stella would say, and that scares the crap out of you."

"You're crazy. It would be insane for two people like us to fall in love. We have nothing in common." He pulls the bag out of my mug and stirs some honey into my tea. Just the way I like it. "I don't know the first thing about relationships or putting someone else first. And you're still recovering from having your heart ripped out."

"I most certainly am not. Richard humiliated me, hurt my pride, but my heart is just fine, thank you very much."

He makes eye contact with me for the first time tonight, and my world shifts. He's looked at me with annoyance. He's looked at me with amusement. He's looked at me with hunger. This is something completely new.

He's never looked at me in love before.

Or maybe I just didn't see it before. Maybe I was too wrapped up in my feelings of inadequacy to notice. And now I can't not see it. The light in his gorgeous eyes when he looks at me. "You're falling for me," I don't realize the words have tumbled out of my mouth until it's too late to scoop them back in.

Panic shadows his face. "No." He shakes his head vehemently. "No, Tru."

"You are," I continue, heedless, I guess. "You are. That's what this is about. You're not trying to protect my heart. You're trying to protect yours."

"Woman, you have been nothing but a trip to Crazy Town since you got here."

"It's all right, Nash. I know this isn't what either of us wanted. We just need to think it through."

I look around the apartment, the home he's welcomed me into. The dogs are cuddled together on a bed. Everything fits. I panic a little. "How did we let this happen?"

"We didn't let anything happen, but I see you are proving my point. I knew you were getting the wrong idea."

I most certainly cannot fall in love. Not now. Not with him. I mean, he's great. Better than great. It's me—I can't be vulnerable. Not again. Not ever again. That doesn't mean I don't get a little flustered with the look of horror in his eyes. "Look, I know why I'm not interested in a relationship. But what exactly is your deal? I mean not just with me, but in general? With relationships?"

"I just never wanted to settle down."

I take a sip of my tea. Again, he's not seeing how settled he is. "But why? Did you have a bad breakup?"

"No."

"Did something happen to you? You never talk about your mother."

"And I'm not going to start tonight. Go to bed, Tru."

Oh, hit a nerve, did I? "Is she...gone?"

"She was never here. Not in any meaningful way. I really am not going into it with you."

At my bland look, he shrugs and sits on the couch, so I join him. "So she's not dead."

"Not that I know of."

Interesting. "Does she live nearby?"

"Tru," he warns.

"You know every sordid thing about my family life. I shared my most humiliating experience with you. I'm not going to be scared off by you telling me you don't want to talk about it."

His voice is clipped, edged with annoyance or anger or both. "My mother was a groupie. Might still be. She followed Ironwing around from bar to bar in Los Angeles, and then when they hit it big, she followed them around from venue to venue. She got knocked up and claimed it was my dad."

"What do you mean claimed?"

"He never asked for a paternity test. He gave her money, a place to stay. Married her. Ironwing stopped touring because he didn't think it would be a good way to raise kids. I think he didn't trust her parenting skills if he wasn't around, and it turns out he was right."

His body is tight with tension, his face squared. I've never seen him like this. Not when he got the dog he didn't want. Not when a stranger showed up and took half of what he'd been working for. Talking about his mother is maybe the only thing that really upsets him.

My hand reaches for his until our fingers link. Hold. "Where is she now?"

"Who knows? She comes back every few years. Gets some money from my dad. Me. Promises she's changed and then ducks out again. She's been pulling that since I was a baby. My dad, he always takes her in. Gets her clean."

Sounds like Brandon. So giving and warm. "Does he still love her?"

"I don't think so. I don't know that he ever did."

I blink once in surprise, and then it hits me. "He takes care of her because he loves you."

His eyes dart to mine. They're cold and dark. "I might not even be his."

"Of course, you are. He loves you. You're his son, Nash. It didn't matter to him then and it doesn't now. Anyone can see how much he loves you."

Nash slumps over. "He gave up music. His whole life. He could have been a rock star. But he gave it all up. For a woman who only used him to get her by, and then kept coming back for more."

I don't want to sound trite, but he needs to know he was worth whatever Brandon might have sacrificed. "Nash, your father gave it up because he wanted to be a dad more than a rock star."

He stands abruptly, prowls the room with too much unspent energy. "Well, anyway, I have no interest in being anyone's Prince Charming."

My head whips up. He's too smart to think all women are like his mother, but I guess he doesn't know he's that smart yet. I do not like being equated with her, though. "Is that what you think I'm looking for? I hate to break it to you, but I don't want to be anyone's damsel in distress. I came here looking to learn how to stand up without the support of a man. If you think for one second, I'm happy about developing feelings for one, you're mistaken. We just need to think this through. Be logical. Neither one of us wants to fall in love, we both recognize the symptoms, so we nip it in the bud."

He narrows his gaze at me. "One of us is falling. I'm just fine."

I nod. "Sure you are." I stand up, determined more than ever to get back on the path I set out from the moment my lawyer informed me of everything Richard had done. "As much as it pains me to say it, you were right about one thing. We can't have sex anymore. We remain professional from here on out." I hold out my hand for a shake. "Deal?"

He stares at my hand. "You think you're just going to stop having feelings for me? Just like that?"

My fake smile dims. "Well, I imagine it might take some time. But once we stop clouding the issue with sex, I see no reason we can't fall right back out."

He shakes my hand warily. "I don't know. Women have more complicated feelings than men. I don't think you're really going to be able to reason with your heart."

"Women do not have more complicated feelings than men. You're being ridiculous. I will get over you just fine. And you will get over me eventually as well."

"I'm not under you."

"Well, not anymore. But that was fun while it lasted."

"Fun while it lasted?"

I scoop up my dildo. "Good night then, Nash. Pleasant dreams."

I wait until I'm in my room to slide down the back of my door and cry. What have I done? How could I be so stupid? The one thing I promised myself I wouldn't ever be again is vulnerable, and I don't know how to rebuild the walls.

TWO WEEKS LATER, I'M sitting at the end of the bar with Stella and her best friend, Perry. We are at the sip portion of our Paint and Sip that Ironwing hosted tonight. Okay, something I hosted through Ironwing at the annoyance of my business partner, who is annoyed by everything lately, so I guess it's not a problem.

Perry nudges me. "You better get down there," she points to the other end of the bar, "it looks like that chick is making a play for your man."

Sure enough, the pretty woman flips her hair, a move I've seen done better by about 85 percent of my sorority sisters. She is pretty, though. I wonder if he likes her.

The idea of it shoots straight to my stomach and burns, but I take a very ladylike sip of my wine. "He's not my man. He's my business partner." I meant to sound professional, but I think it squeaked out of me.

Perry snorts. "Whatever." Perry is an interesting woman. She's one of three lawyers in town. She's gorgeous. Intelligent. And mostly mean.

She's nice to me. And mostly nice to her friends. But she's vicious when she wants to be and I think everyone is afraid of her. She's the exact opposite of Stella, who is concentrating on the tarot cards in front of her.

"What did you draw? The King of Spades or something?" Perry asks her.

Stella shakes her head. "No. There is no King of Spades in the tarot deck." She pushes a card around so it's facing Perry. "This is the Tower. I have pulled it a couple days in a row. I can't figure it out."

"Well, your card isn't going anywhere, but Nash might be," Perry says. "He's getting snared by a tourist."

"What?" Stella asks, looking up, her eyes sharp on the woman. "Who is that?"

"Nobody knows. But the poet here claims she isn't concerned."

"I'm not concerned. He can flirt with whoever he wants."

Stella and Perry exchange looks. "Yeah, we've been wanting to talk to you about that. When are you two going to get together? The guys at the firehall have extended their pool to include the rest of us townies, and I feel like you two owe me inside information."

I close my eyes and take a deep breath, indulging the wish for just a second, and then remember that's not what I want. It's probably just that he got me interested in sex and now I'm not having any.

"Stella, we aren't going to get together. Nash and I are much better as friends, and neither of us want a relationship. Especially with each other."

"Fine, maybe I'll go out with him then," Perry says easily, watching me gleefully like I'm a bomb about to detonate. When I don't satisfy her lust for drama, she leans forward, propping her hands on her chin and bats her eyelashes at Nash.

The face he makes looks like indigestion, and he turns his back to us, still talking to the tourist.

"I think I might be the only one of my friends who hasn't slept with him yet," she says, not even upset that he's ignoring her.

"Gross!" Stella says. "I haven't slept with him. In fact, who are you even talking about? He's never...oh," she pauses at the look on Perry's face. "I was supposed to play along with that, wasn't I?"

"Really, both of you can stop. We have acknowledged that there is an attraction between us..." A mind-numbing attraction. "...but have decided to stay professional." I look over and see he's got the woman's phone in his hands. Is he giving her his phone number? In front of me? Really?

What a fool I've been. I just assumed that he would have the courtesy to not rub it in my face that he was already moving on. I thought...it doesn't matter what I thought.

"It's different for men, isn't it?" I ask rhetorically but hoping someone has an answer.

"I'm so sorry," Stella says, as we all watch Nash watch in appreciation as the woman who got his number sashays to the door, looking over her shoulder once to execute another hair flip.

"God, that move should be outlawed," Perry says. "It's so cliché."

What is cliché is falling for the first man to pay attention to me...twice.

Chapter Nine

Nash

Tru has been acting strangely since last night at the bar. Well, stranger than normal.

When I get back from a trip to my dad's to help him move some furniture, my chest hollows out the moment I open the apartment door.

She's gone.

I can feel it.

I swallow and stand there, one foot over the threshold, the other stubbornly clinging to the hall. It won't be real if I don't go in.

What's wrong with me? I wanted this, right? My quiet life back. My old patterns resumed.

I rub my chest, surprised at the sharp pain beneath my ribs.

Stella opens her apartment door behind me. "Oh, good. You're home. I have to go and I was going to have to bring your dog with me." She hands me the end of Bo's leash and he pays no attention to me because he's slathering to get into our apartment thinking his girl is in there. "Perry tried a charcoal mask and can't get it off. She's crying." She holds up her phone so I can see a picture of Perry with mud all over her face. Women are so weird. "I have to go help her. And take more pictures and maybe a video. Anyway, take your dog and call Tru and say whatever you need to get her home. I mean it, Nash. She was really good for you." She reaches up and kisses my cheek. "Normally, I'd be all up in your face about this but I have a feeling you're already going to feel pretty shitty without my help. Plus, nobody ever gets to see Perry cry, so I don't want to miss it. Do the right thing and call Tru. Love you."

She's down the stairs before I can even respond. I look down at my dog and he's staring at me like I'm an idiot. He's one to talk.

"You're right. I am an idiot. Why am I standing in the hall when I just got my life back?"

We go inside and he runs around sniffing everywhere trying to find Fifi. The guest room door is open, the bed made, the dresser and nightstand empty.

My heartbeat thickens when I see paper on the kitchen counter. Did she leave me a note?

The closer I get, I see it's typed. Numbered paragraphs and indemnities and clauses. I go to the last page and see her signature.

She signed over her percentage of Ironwing to me.

She's gone.

I LAST TWO DAYS BEFORE I ask my dad, "How's Tru doing?"

He lowers the paper enough to level a frown at me. "Why don't you ask Tru?"

"She doesn't want to hear from me."

"I'm sure she'd love to hear from you."

"She changed her number."

He goes back to the paper. "Did she?"

He knows damn well she did. "Bo misses Fifi."

"That's too bad. Poor dog."

I push down the newspaper. "Give me a break, Pops."

"She's fine. Fifi is fine."

I grab a glass and start polishing. "Great. Glad to hear it."

"Give me a break, son."

I walk away, fill the peanuts, polish another glass. I'm glad she's fine. Really. Nice to know she's doing just fine without me. "Hey, old man. If she asks about me, make sure you tell her I'm fine too."

"Heh," he huffs. "You're a mess."

"I am not." I stalk back toward him. "Things are getting back to normal. Just the way I like it."

"Good for you, son."

I tear the newspaper out of his hands. Well, the half that comes with the motion. He's still holding on to the bottom piece. "You seem fine to me," he says blandly.

"I'm just worried about her. I feel responsible. You know. I want to make sure she's got someplace to stay. Enough to get by."

"Let me ask you something. If you care so much about her, why didn't you tell her you cared while she was here?"

"Tru and I were friends. Business partners. We weren't dating or anything."

Damn. He's looking right through me. "If you care so much about her, why didn't you date her?"

"You know me. I'm not the boyfriend kind of guy."

He takes a long drink of his coffee. I don't know how he stomachs the stuff. "Why aren't you the boyfriend kind of guy?"

I shrug. "Just never wanted to settle down." His dad-stare just bores into me. "I'm a rolling stone."

"I think you're a chicken shit."

"Pops!"

"Well, you are. I've seen a lot of really nice women float in and out of your life, and you stay friends with all of them. Something scares you about letting them in, though."

Lord save me if he decides to write a song about me. It would be just my luck that Ironwing gets back together. He's still staring at me. "I just don't want anyone to depend on me to save them."

"Save them? Son, is this about your mom?"

I blow out a breath. "I really don't want to talk about her."

"Maybe it's time we do."

The last time I saw her, she didn't look well. And she stole my car. "I'm selfish enough to be glad that you're the man who stepped in and took care of me. But I'm also selfish enough to never want to be the guy that gives up his dream for some woman and her drama."

"I didn't give up anything for your mother or her drama. If this is about Ironwing, you know I don't regret breaking up the band to be a better father."

"Jake already had a kid when you were touring. He didn't think he had to quit."

"Jake had Miranda. She was his grade-school crush. She was a great mom and Leo had a stable home here. I knew your mom couldn't be counted on to handle things when I was on the road. Hell, she loved being on the road more than all of us put together. I didn't like it all that much. It was fun for a time, but I'm a family man at heart."

My gaze catches that damn mirror she bought with the Ironwing logo on it. "You shouldn't have had to choose one or the other."

He rests his hand over mine. It's still always a little jarring to see our hands together and mine be the same size. My eyes always expect the big dad hand I held to cross the street. "I didn't give anything up for your mother. I did the best I could for her. But it was always about you, son. I thought you knew that. Finding out I was going to be a dad was the best thing that ever happened to me. I never considered it a sacrifice to come home to Brazen Bay and watch you grow."

Oh, hell. I don't want to have feelings right now. Shit. It feels like an orange is sitting in my throat. "I love you, old man."

"Back-attcha. But I still think you're chicken shit."

I laugh, which is better than the stupid tears I'm fighting back. Why does talking to my dad sometimes make me feel like a little boy? "Thanks."

"Your mom has a lot of problems. But she loves you, even if she doesn't know how." He pats my hand. "Most people have a better idea of how to love someone. Probably every woman you never took a chance on, even."

I run my tongue around my teeth and stifle the denial that wants to burst out. Because he's right. Damn it. I am a chicken shit. And it's too late to fix things with Tru. When a woman changes her phone number to avoid you, it's too late. I'm not going to stalk her.

I nod at my dad. "Next time you hear from Tru, please tell her I asked how she's doing."

"And how should I tell her you are if she asks?"

She won't ask.

"Tell her I'm fine."

Tru

THE DOORBELL RINGS, Fifi barks, and Pauline pauses fixing her makeup in the entryway mirror and looks like she's going to throw up. "Oh, God. He's here."

I smile warmly. "You look fantastic." She looks a little green, actually, but her outfit is on point and it will take Brandon a minute to look up from her chest anyway.

"Are you sure it's okay to leave Danny with you? I can cancel...I don't want you to feel like you have to—"

"I'm happy to babysit Danny." And I am. "I'm going to answer the door. Pull yourself together, woman." It's their first official date, though she and Brandon have been hanging out as friends all this time.

"Shush, Fifi." I open up the apartment door and hug Brandon. Fifi bounces around his legs happily. She's very fond of him, like most females.

"Hey, Tru. Is she ready?"

"Of course not. Come in. Can I get you something while you wait?"

"Nope. I'm happy to wait as long as it takes."

"How's everyone?" It's been weeks since I left Brazen Bay and Ironwing to stay at Pauline's.

"Everyone is fine, Tru. Just fine."

Right. They probably forgot about me already anyway. I was barely a blip on their radar.

"That Spuds McKenzie beer light you ordered showed up. It looks great. Nash hung it up right away. Said he liked it."

"No, he didn't."

"No. I hung it up when he wasn't looking. But he hasn't taken it down yet, so that's something."

Before I left, I was thinking that we needed to make Ironwing more '80s themed. It already had the vibe, but I figured we should play it up more. I'd been scouting memorabilia and trying to come up with theme nights.

But I don't need to think about it anymore, do I? Ironwing and its owner can languish away in the obscurity he likes so much.

Pauline makes her grand entrance and the tension between the two of them is making me sweat. If I were still in Brazen Bay, one of the guys from the firehall would make a bet about whether or not they were going to make their dinner reservation or just go get a hotel.

"You look beautiful," he says. She looks a little like the women who danced on a car in his music video. Which is probably what she was going for.

Pauline turns to me. She's blinking a lot, which is the only way I can tell she's still super nervous. "I wrote down everything I could think of on a pad by the phone. Don't let him have more screen time than he's allowed or he won't sleep."

"I know. I live here now, remember?"

"Right. And his pediatrician's number is on there. And—"

Brandon wraps her coat around her shoulders. "I'm sure Tru can handle it."

"Sorry. I just…"

He cups her chin. "If you don't think I was the biggest worrier every time I left Nash with a sitter, you don't know me well enough yet. I was the worst."

My heart pings at his name. But I'm getting better. Really I am.

Two hours later, I am tucking Danny into his toddler bed when he asks me why I don't have any kids. Fifi settles in at the foot of his bed. She sleeps with him on the nights his mom has to work. Some sort of unspoken agreement between Danny and my dog.

I ruffle his hair. "Not everyone gets to be as lucky as your mom."

If anyone else heard me stay that, they might think I am jealous because she had a child with my ex-husband and I didn't. But Danny doesn't know that backstory. He just knows I like him.

"You should have one. Then I'd have a new friend. You'd be a good mommy."

"You think so?" I tuck his sheet around him tightly, the way he likes it. "Why is that?"

"You smell nice and you read good stories."

I wonder if that's all it really takes to be a good mom. I don't really remember mine, but my grandmother also smelled nice and read good stories. I may not have grown up with the most traditional family, but they loved me. I could love someone like that. Now isn't a great time, but someday, I could maybe adopt a child. "Get some rest, bug. Your mom told me we can have waffles in the morning."

He frowns a little. "You're not making them, are you?"

"No, of course not. Mommy made the rule, remember?"

He looks relieved. It was just a small fire, and in my defense, well, I have no defense. I've given up on cooking and promised Pauline I would stick to microwave soup and sandwiches.

I'm dozing on the couch when the door opens. I sit up and rub my eyes, surprised to see a man sneaking in. I blink a few times. No. It can't be.

"Richard?"

Chapter Ten

Tru

He's lost a lot of weight. Too much for his frame. And he's got a beard. I don't think he's shaved or gotten a haircut since I last saw him. So unlike the meticulous man I married.

"Richard?" I repeat. That may be all I'm capable of right now. What is he doing here? I figured he'd be lazing around on an island somewhere collecting more wives and a tan.

"What are you doing here?" he asks, clearly just as stunned as I am. Of course, he was expecting wife number one, not wife number two. "Where's Pauline? What have you done with her?"

My nerves are jumping on the trampoline of my stomach right now. I don't know that I could have prepared myself to see him, but being surprised by seeing him is a cruel twist of fate. "Pauline isn't here. And if she were, she would not want to see you."

He pushes past me, barging in and looking around the room. "Is she all right?"

"Do you think I hurt her?" His bloodshot eyes dart around. Is he on drugs now too? "I see. You think a woman scorned and all that. Well, sorry to disappoint you, but I actually like Pauline more than I liked you. We're roommates."

"Roommates?" He shakes his head. "Whatever. I don't have time for this. Where is she? Where's my son?"

Now that the shock is wearing off, I'm remembering what a flea he is. "Whatever? Are you even serious right now? That's what you have to say to me? Not, 'I'm sorry I stole your inheritance, Tru?' Not, 'I feel really bad that I was still married to someone else when I tricked you into marrying me, Tru?' Not, 'I'm the worst kind of human for pretending to care about your grandfather?"

He scratches his beard roughly. Maybe he really does have fleas. "I honestly cared about your grandfather. He was a good man."

"And yet you deceived him and stole his money while his corpse was still warm."

I've probably imagined this moment a thousand times. All the things I would say, finally, after he robbed me of closure. And all my money. I had a million zingers lined up. And boy was I ever going to slap his face, soap-opera style.

And now that he's here, all I want is for him to go away and leave us alone. He isn't sorry. He won't ever be sorry. And he never even cared for me a little. He hasn't even asked if I'm all right.

"Where's my son?"

Those trampoline jumping nerves skate up to the back of my neck, my instincts sharpen, and I start trying to remember where I set my phone. This is no longer about me. He's not a good man when he's being himself, and right now, Richard is unhinged. I can't let him get anywhere near little Danny.

"He's with Pauline."

He stares into my eyes, narrowing them to slits while he tries to decide his next move. "I'll wait."

"I don't think so. I want you to leave."

He grabs my wrist. "Don't make me do something neither of us want me to do. I want my son. I'm not leaving here without him. If you try to get in my way, I'll stop you. Any way I have to."

"You're hurting me, Richard. Let go," I tell him calmly, but my heart is beating too fast. He drops my wrist, but doesn't back away. The last thing I need is for him to lose it. "You don't look well, Richard. When was the last time you ate?" I ask, feigning concern.

He shakes his head. "I don't know. Yesterday."

"If you won't leave, at least sit down. I'll make you a sandwich."

He sits on the couch, watching me warily. I'm not completely hidden from view in the kitchen, since it's all open concept in the apartment, but I swipe my phone and dial 911 while gathering sandwich supplies.

I can't talk to the operator, but I hope that keeping them on the line is the best solution. "How did you even find us, Richard?" I ask, hoping the phone is picking up my voice. "Pauline said she moved so you wouldn't know where she lived? And the Terrace Court Apartment Complex is a secure building."

I know they can't hear him. But I hope they are at least trying. "She can't keep my son from me."

"But you're a wanted criminal now. What will you do with a four-year-old boy?"

"He's my son. She's my wife. We belong together."

Bastard. I bet he just needs the money back that he gave her before he left. He's obviously lost the rest of it somehow. Still, the thought of him on the run with little Danny makes my hands shake. I try to control that when I hand him his plate.

"How did you even become friends?" he asks me, smelling the bread for poison. Damn. Why didn't I think of poison?

"She found me. She wanted me to know she didn't know about me, either. When you married me."

Danny starts talking in his sleep, loud enough for his voice to carry into the living room and Richard stands up and starts for his bedroom door. "You lying bitch."

I race in the same direction, getting in front of him and shoving as hard as I can. I hear Fifi growling on the other side of the door. I hope she doesn't wake up Danny. I don't want him to be scared, and his dad looks anything but safe right now. "You are not taking Danny."

"What do you care, Tru?"

"I love that little boy. And I love Pauline. And you are done wrecking our lives."

He smiles. How had I not noticed he was missing a tooth? A life on the run has not been a picnic for the flea. Good. "You've changed. Not enough. What a boring little twat you were."

He tries to push past me, but I'm done being passive. I grab him and headbutt him, hearing a satisfying crack and hoping it wasn't my skull, then I knee him in the balls. He drops instantly, moaning. "Pauline and I started a self-defense class at the gym once a week, asshole." I kick him in the stomach. "Also, you have a tiny penis and don't know what a clitoris is."

I scrabble over him to get to the phone just as the door opens and Brandon and Pauline come in. Pauline's eyes widen and Brandon strides across the room.

"Is that Richard?" she asks.

I nod. The police are at the door before I can tell her everything, and after, getting Brandon to leave would take an act of God, so we put him on the couch and I go to bed.

Not ten minutes later, Pauline knocks and comes in with two glasses and a box of wine. "I'm too wired to sleep." She sets the box on my dresser and pours our glasses. "I'm so glad you made sure that 'you have a tiny penis and don't know what a clitoris is' made it into the police report."

I grin, welcoming her onto my bed where we sit cross-legged and drink our very classy vintage. "I'm hoping it gets read aloud at his hearing."

"I can't believe he found us...that he even looked for us. I thought he was long gone."

"He looked terrible, didn't he?"

"I can't believe I married him."

"I can't believe I married him, either."

We both laugh at that. If someone had told me a year ago that I'd be laughing about being married to a bigamist with my sister wife after having taken him down with a headbutt and knee to the groin, I'd have laughed all the way back to my penthouse.

Alone. Lonely. With only Fifi to hear the tale.

My life is actually so much better. Almost. I'm so grateful to have Pauline and Danny in my life, but I miss Nash.

Don't go there.

As many times as I imagined finally telling Richard off, it's nothing compared to the millions of times a day I think of Nash. Of course, he stars in all my sexual fantasies, but I find myself wishing I could tell him things about my day all the time. Wishing I could hear his voice, be danced around the room by him, work side by side with him. And then I remember the last time I saw him and know that I could never work side by side with him and watch him move on with his life with a front row seat.

Pauline bumps my knee, dragging me out of my sad, sad spiral. "Seriously, though. Thank you for protecting my son." She grabs my hand and squeezes. "I can never repay you."

"You and Danny are my family now."

"Well, you're ours too. But you know, we aren't the only ones who love you. Brandon says everyone in Brazen Bay misses you."

I shrug. "It was a great town. But not for me." Except for the fact that I loved everything about it.

She studies me over the rim of her glass. "Brandon thinks of you like a daughter. Which is weird since I think of you as a sister and I'm dating him."

"Brandon is great. How did the date go?"

"Wonderful. Don't change the subject."

"I thought we were talking about Brandon?"

"You know perfectly well we were not talking about Brandon. When are you going to call Nash?"

I down my glass. "I'm not going to call Nash."

"He never went out with that woman."

I send her a sharp look. "It's not my business who he dates or doesn't date."

"He gave her his number in the bar that night because she sells memorabilia and had one of his dad's guitars from a show they did at the Viper Room. He finally told Stella the truth that he wanted to make you jealous, so he didn't deny—"

"It really doesn't matter. That woman isn't going to be the last to get his phone number. He didn't want to care about me, and I can't watch him date other people."

"Did you ever tell him that you changed your mind and you want to care about him? Because last I heard, he didn't know."

Technically, the last conversation we had was about how easy it was going to be for us to get over each other. "It doesn't matter, Pauline. I need to learn how to survive without a man."

"Oh, but honey, men are so much fun." She gets up for more wine, offering to take my glass, but I shake my head. "Nash loves you. He's miserable without you."

"Oh, did he admit that to Stella also?"

"No. But everyone knows it."

Right.

I yawn, exaggerating the stretch that goes with it. "I'm really tired. Taking down a fleabag was a lot of work."

Pauline sighs. "I get it. I get it." She pauses by the door. "Do you love him?"

"The fleabag?"

"Don't be stupid."

Nash. "Maybe. Probably. Yes. But it doesn't change anything."

"I'm sorry to hear that. We'll dissect my date tomorrow, yeah?"

I smile, my heart warmed over by the happy look in her eye. "I can't wait."

MONDAY MORNING, PAULINE and I are sitting on the bench behind the prosecuting attorney's table at the courthouse waiting for Richard's arraignment. We squeeze each other's hand when they bring him in wearing prison sweats and handcuffs.

This is just one step. What happens today only determines whether or not he'll wait for trial in a cell or if they will release him, ensuring he'll run again.

Someone sits at the end of our row and it looks like...Perry? I turn and notice that several rows are filled with familiar faces. Stella, Brandon, Leo, Dixie, even Stella's sister, Megan, is here. I look over my other shoulder and catch Nash's gaze. He gives me an encouraging nod and I'm flooded with warmth.

"They came," I whisper to Pauline. I've felt so blessed just to have Pauline and Danny stick with me that it never occurred to me that the people I met in Brazen Bay would be here for us too.

She turns and waves when she sees Brandon. "Wow. I've only been to that town three times. They're here for you, honey."

"You're dating the town's lead singer, who is crazy about you. I'm guessing they're here for you too."

The judge comes in, we all rise, and then I pray that they don't let him out. He'll run away and he might still try to get Danny. He's got nothing to lose now. Which is why I'm shocked when he pleads guilty.

The whole thing is over and done with so fast I can barely process it. They take him back to the county jail, and I sit there blinking. "C'mon," Pauline nudges. "They're going to call the next case and I don't want to get stuck here."

We filter out into the hall, Pauline gravitating to Brandon right away. I turn toward the steps to see Nash coming down. He stops right where he is, one foot still on the bottom step. For a moment, we just stare at each other in this strange instant of time slowing down. His mouth curves around a slow smile, and my stomach tumbles the way it always does around him.

"Wow," Dixie says, somehow sneaking up by my side, snapping my awareness back to the present. "That woman sure knows how to wear a dress."

She's looking at Pauline in the blue dress that molds against her curves, but shows very little skin for Pauline. "Yes, that's her demure courtroom dress. I talked her out of red."

Dixie hugs me. "How are you?"

"Better today. How are the wedding plans?"

"Oh my gosh. Please don't ask. Megan is here and if you get her started...anyway, I just wanted to make sure you were coming on Friday. We're having a very small, informal engagement party at Ironwing."

"I thought that was next week."

"Nope. This Friday. Promise me you'll come."

I turn to the stairs, but Nash isn't there. "It might be weird. I don't want to make your party awkward."

"You have to promise me you'll come. Almost everyone there is a Brazen Bay native. I need your support."

"I'll try."

"You promise."

"I promise I'll try."

She hugs me again. "I'm glad your ex is stuck behind bars. I'll see you Friday."

I get hugs and well wishes from everyone, as well as admonishments to show up on Friday, so I guess I'm going to get closure on more than just the flea this week.

Chapter Eleven

Nash

Ironwing is awfully dead for a Friday.

Is it a holiday I don't know about? Something catches my notice outside and it's...a woman pacing the sidewalk outside the bar again.

Tru? I want to know what she's doing, but I also just want to watch her for a minute. I didn't get my fill of looking at her on Monday, and seeing her here, in Brazen Bay, in front of Ironwing, makes my nerves hum.

I rub my now sweaty palms on my jeans and open the door. "Are you protesting something? I knew I should have made a sandwich board for you that day."

A flush creeps into her cheeks. She's so pretty it's impossible to be real. "I'm working up my nerve."

"And how is that going?"

"Not great."

"You look great, Gertrude. Really, you look amazing."

She moistens her lips and darts a shy sideways glance at me. "Thank you. And thank you for coming to the arraignment. It meant a lot to see you there."

My hands are itching to hold her. Grab her. Maybe throw her over my shoulder and bring her home where she belongs. But just because I've figured out what I want, what I need, doesn't mean I get to have it.

"Are you coming in?"

"Is everyone already in there?"

"Everyone?" That's when I see the sign on the door reading *Closed for private party*. It all becomes a little more clear to me. Why Stella was standing in front of the door earlier right after my dad walked out. The whispers. Damn meddling town.

Tru steps into the dark, quiet pub. "I don't understand. Dixie told me the party was tonight. Pauline told me she'd catch up with me. Did they...they set us up?"

"Looks like it." I spend about five minutes asking her inane questions just to keep her here. Keep her talking. When she asks me how my baseball team is doing, I know we've taken small talk too far.

"I should go."

"No, wait. I, ah, I need your help with something."

"All right."

"I need your help planning an engagement party."

I've seen that face. It's the one she uses when she's trying to do math in her head. "I thought Megan was planning Dixie and Leo's party."

"She is. I need your help with a different one."

"Nash, you hated all the events I planned."

"I never meant to make you feel like that. The truth is the bar was better when you were here. I've been doing a lot of the things you wrote on the business plan you left. They're solid."

She beams like someone just crowned her Miss America. "Thank you."

"This party has to be perfect."

"I've never planned an engagement party before but if I get any ideas, I guess I can call you. Who is getting married?"

"I am."

Her smiled dims and the color drains from her face. "Oh. You want me to help you plan your engagement party." Her eyes cool and she goes aloof. "Who are you marrying?"

"Well, I haven't gotten her to say yes yet. It isn't going to be easy. She's been hurt before and I've made a mess of things."

"I don't think I'm the right person to help you."

I point to the wall where a plastic sandwich bag is filled with scraps of paper inside a shadow box. "Do you see that?" When she looks, I tell her, "That's the contract I never signed. The one where you gave me your portion of the bar. Ironwing is still yours. Mostly."

"You didn't...what does this have to do with getting married? Are you leaving Brazen Bay, too?"

"How do you think I should ask her? She's so beautiful and smart, and she knows a lot of romance language stuff and poetry, I'm only good at plain speak. Boring words."

She whips her head back to me. I wait a beat.

"I've done just about everything wrong with her. Made a real ass out of myself."

She swallows hard. "Well, to be fair, you are an ass. It would be unfair to expect otherwise." She's trying to read my expression. "She's probably not perfect, either. Maybe the two of you can come to an understanding. You should use your plain, boring words. I'm sure that's what she'd prefer."

"Should I get down on one knee?"

"Um, well, if she's nervous, she might need you to hold her up. Maybe put your hands on her hips, like this." She places my hands on her hips and my heart starts thudding in my ears.

"Like this?"

She nods. "Yeah. And then maybe she would put her arms around you. For support. Like this." She loops her arms around my neck and her eyes lift to my face.

"And then just tell her that I need her? That my life is shit without her?"

"I'm sure she'd like to hear that."

I wonder what she would do if I pressed my lips to hers. "Should I tell her that I think she's literally the bravest person I've ever met? That I'm in awe of the way she just tackles whatever life hands her, even when she's scared? That I'm the one who needs to learn how to be courageous?"

"She might not believe you."

"It's true. I shut out anything that might change my life because I was afraid to take a chance on making it better. My life was fine, but it wasn't good, Tru, not until you came into it."

Here goes nothing.

I take one hand off her hip and pull a ring out of my pocket.

Her eyes round with shock. "My grandmother's ring...how did you..."

"Perry helped me track down your lawyer. He gave us a lead on some of your personal things. Some of the liquidated items were sold off to different places, but I found this still in New York. You told me once it was the only thing you wished you could get back."

"I can't believe you did that for me. This means so much to me, to see it again. Thank you."

"It's yours, even if you say no, it's yours. But if you say yes, it's just the beginning. We can build something great together. Say you'll marry me."

Her eyes cloud with confusion. "I want to say yes, but don't you want to date for a while first? It seems so rash, so sudden."

"I don't want to wait. I will if you want to, but I've been living my life in neutral long enough."

"Wait, did you know about this setup today? Why did you have the ring in your pocket?'

I chuckle. "I always have the ring in my pocket. But I was planning on getting you alone next week, at the real party. Maybe tying you to my bed until you said yes."

Her eyes twinkle with mischief. "Is that still an option?"

My dick swells at the thought. "Say yes, Gertrude."

"If I say yes, you promise to tie me to your bed?"

"I promise."

"Can Fifi be in the wedding?"

"You're killing me. Please say yes. Please say...shit. I knew I would screw this up. I love you. I didn't say that yet. I love you. And I love your stupid rat-like dog. And I love the terrible, wonderful things you do to my bar. I missed you so damn much and I really want to tie you to my bed, so hurry and say yes so I can lock this damn door. We're closed for a private party."

"I love you, too. If you can wait to marry me until I get my MBA, then yes."

"You want to wait?"

"We can live in sin and have obnoxious sex whenever you want—but I want to finish school before I plan a wedding. And Megan is not getting near any of the planning."

I slide the ring on her finger and the rest of my life begins.

Epilogue

Nash

Two Years Later

When my fiancée enters the balloon-festooned bar, it takes me a minute to recognize her. Or anyone she's with. She's wearing a tight neon pink dress, purple eyeshadow, and ankle boots with lace socks. The rest looks similar. Big hair, lots of ruffles and lace.

She crosses the room to me and I have to ask, "Babe, is that you?" as I lean down for a quick kiss. Tru doesn't wear tight dresses as a rule, which is fine by me since I know what's under all her conservative, prim and proper attire. But this side of her is also more than fine with me. I'm barely managing to keep my tongue in my mouth. The dress is molded to all her curves, short and snug. She's all legs and silky skin. And mine. She's all mine.

The heat coils low in my belly, making me forget we're not alone. I kiss her again, slower this time. She's sweet and hot, and she moans quietly until I hear someone clear their throat behind us.

Whoops. "Sorry."

"No, you're not."

"I am so. I'm sorry we're not alone. I'm sorry that I can't haul you over my shoulder and take you home or at least into the office." I reach out to touch her hair and she flinches.

"Please don't touch it."

"How did you even...build that?" I ask about her hairstyle which looks tall, crimpy, and crunchy.

"Aqua Net and YouTube."

"Do you know how you're going to tear it down?"

She shakes her head. "I'm a little nervous about it. But I figure women still had hair in the '90s after living through the '80s, so one night of damage might be okay. What do you think of the bar?"

I look around and take in the '80s prom theme decorations for our engagement party. "It's ridiculous. I love it."

I myself am wearing a tuxedo with a hot pink bow tie and cummerbund that matches Tru's dress. I find Leo when Tru gets called away. He's similarly attired and looks as uncomfortable as I do.

"Jesus," he starts. "I can't even tell you how worried I was my dad was going to bring out the assless chaps for this thing."

"I knew mine wasn't going to wear Spandex, but I did have to talk him out of wearing a tuxedo he actually saved from his prom. He insisted that it still fit him. He would have split his pants down the back the first time he bent over."

"Sort of like assless chaps then."

We toast each other's beer and look at our women across the room.

"Your wife is as big as a house, man."

He smiles. "Twins."

"No shit?"

"Just found out today."

I shudder. I want kids, even though that's scary as shit. But I don't want two at once. Mostly I just want to practice making them.

Leo seems to like being a dad. They already have one. "Remember three years ago when we shared a flask in the parking lot of the Masonic Temple while we were hiding out from the garter toss at your cousin's wedding?"

"Now look at us."

I shake my head and take another drink of beer. "We're caged and shackled now. No more sowing wild oats. No more freedom."

Leo is still looking at his wife. "It's fucking awesome, isn't it?"

I laugh. "It's the best. What surprised you the most about being married?"

"Thinking it wouldn't change anything to have the piece of paper and finding out it changed everything. Everything is better. You'll see."

"Looking forward to it." I can't wait to be married, something I never thought I'd say.

We're also celebrating Tru's MBA tonight. She's worked really hard. I love watching the way she glows from all the people wishing us well. She fits here. I've never been prouder of this podunk town than when they all made room for her to be here.

We're about an hour into the party when Pops takes the stage. Tru thinks he's going to give a toast, but when Jake Stone and the rest of Ironwing go up on stage with him, she looks at me with confusion clouding her gaze.

I take her hand and lead her to the dance floor. Pops holds up his glass and gets the mic. "The day Gertrude Stanhope walked into this bar was one of the happiest days of my life. You might wonder why—I mean, she was here to take my son's bar away from him." Everyone chuckles. "But I knew as soon as I saw her. I got to witness the moment my son fell in love. I've never been prouder of my boy than when he learned how to give his heart away. Tru brought a lot to us when she came to Brazen Bay—my own wife," he waves to Pauline, "a *nearly* profitable bar for my son, friendship to so many, and she reminded a few old guys that their glory days don't need to be behind them."

"What is he talking about?" she asks me quietly.

"Just listen."

Someone brings up some instruments and my dad continues talking. "We're not quite ready for a reunion tour, but we've been practicing something special for you, Tru."

She brings her fingers to her lips and her eyes well up with tears when they play an acoustic version of their one-hit wonder, "Bold." When the chorus starts, the whole bar starts singing along, like they always do. The moment is so damn sweet I need a filling, but I squeeze my girl and sing along. It's the most ridiculous song in the whole world. But it's ours. This song, this band, this bar, this town, these people.

Leo and Dixie come around with trays of sparkling wine and we endure toast after toast. After the fourth one, I notice Tru's glass is still full.

"Why aren't you drinking your wine? Do you have a headache?"

She shakes her head and lifts her glass when Stella finishes a long rambling ode to our dogs, who we put in the office so no one would give them cake. People always try to give them cake when they start drinking.

Tru pretends to sip from her glass. "No, I'm fine. Just don't feel like drinking."

I take her glass from her hand and down it quickly, suddenly parched. I can't think, can't clear my mind. My heart clenches and my pulse is pounding and I look at her, really look at her. She really is glowing. It's not the makeup, it's not the lighting. I pull her into me for a crushing hug. "You're pregnant?" I say, my voice raw and my throat too thick.

She nods and her crunchy hair scratches my eyeball, but I don't even care. Holy shit. She's pregnant.

"Everybody out," I holler. "She's having my baby."

Of course that means more toasts and hugs, and fuck me, will these people go home already? I need to be alone with her. I need to be inside of her.

Why did we rent the old apartment when we moved? I mean our new house is great, but come on, we could be in bed in two minutes if we still lived above the bar. Instead, I have to endure another hour of our friends, a ten-minute drive, and who made the sidewalk to my front door so long?

We're finally in the damn door. "Please don't break my hair," is all she says when she sees the look in my eyes, then she's whimpering because I've already pulled her dress and bra down to get my mouth on her round, juicy breasts. She goes boneless, so I scoop her up and bring her to the big chair. She's on my lap, squirming, grinding against my hard cock. The hem of her dress bunches easily in my hand while she works on my zipper, freeing me.

Not going to lie, she looks pretty slutty all made up with her dress around her middle, her luscious tits swaying as she moves her hips seductively. I still her hips so I can move her panties to the side and position my cock right where we both want it. Need it. I tease her with it, rubbing myself where she's so wet, so ready for me.

When I slide home, her back arches, thrusting her chest out. I take a nipple in my mouth and suck hard, but hold perfectly still below the waist until she starts panting and trying to move, trying to fuck me if I won't fuck her.

"Patience."

She rests her forehead against mine. "Please, Nash."

"I want to make it last, Gertrude."

"Oh, really?" she asks, squeezing her inner muscles until my cock twitches involuntarily. "You want to take your time?"

I grunt roughly, the sweat pooling at my temples. I'm on the edge of a mind-blowing climax already. I can't get close enough, can't get enough of her in my arms, my hands. I kiss her, stroking my tongue against hers, wanting to be inside her any way I can. My entire body is thrumming for action.

"I must be more turned on than you, I guess," she says when she comes up for air, biting my lower lip. "Because knowing you knocked me up has made me so horny, Nash. You put a *baby* in me."

I can't stop the groan that barrels out of me, but I squeeze her hips to hold her still. "Jesus, why is that so hot?"

She can't move the way she wants, so she brings her hand to my chest and pinches my nipple hard enough that I see stars and suck in a harsh breath, letting go of her hips and finding her hands, lacing our fingers together. "You play dirty."

"I'm a dirty, dirty girl." She rocks her hips and I meet her with a jolting thrust. "Again, do that again."

Over and over, I pump into her. I lose my vision at some point. My hearing too. All I know is the dark, pulsing rhythm that surrounds us from the inside out. She's everything I never wanted. And more.

She's writhing now, reaching for that peak, and when her inner walls start convulsing around me, we shatter at the same time.

I'm not shackled. Not caged. But I used to be. I used to live in a world where I thought I had to keep my heart under lock and key.

And now I'm free.

DEAR READER,

I love that Nash thought he was grumpier than anyone else did. Next up is Stella's book, and boy is she fun to write.

If you enjoyed *The Right Stuff*, please consider leaving a review at your favorite vendor so other readers like you can find it.

Until Next Time,

Brilly

[1]

---

1. https://www.bookbub.com/authors/brill-harper

2

WHAT WOULD YOU DO IF the boyfriend you totally made up to get your sister off your back showed up at your place of employment?

Free-spirited Stella Stone has always been the wild child in her family, but even she is surprised at the amount of trouble she's found herself in this time.

Christopher Lockwood was a random name she chose from the internet. How was she supposed to know he would end taking a temporary position in the veterinary office she manages? Now she somehow has to keep the uptight, tie-wearing, self-contained Christopher from figuring out that the whole town thinks they are dating, and somehow also keep the whole town from figuring out she's a pathetic liar with a fake boyfriend.

Oh, and it doesn't help that he's a major hottie under those Clark Kent glasses and stern demeanor. In fact,

---

something about his need for control brings out Stella's inner brat, especially when he decides she needs a little discipline.

Too bad there's no such thing as a secret in Brazen Bay. Not for very long.

Author's Confession: This is the most opposite-y opposites attract book ever made even more fun by a fake relationship trope. Stella is a fan favorite and Christopher is the Alpha Nerd Hero you didn't know you needed in your life. You are going to love the surprisingly dirty dude under the restrained and inhibited mask he shows the world. I mean *unf*, am I right? He's the only one who could keep up with our deliciously nutty Stella and give her a worthy HEA.

Excerpt of *So Wrong It's Right*

Stella

YOU KNOW HOW THEY SAY you should learn something new every day? Well, today I learned that there is a big difference between baklava and bukkake.

One is appropriate for dessert at a wedding shower and the other is a word I'm not even sure why I know. (That's a lie. The answer is porn.) But I offered the wrong one as a suggestion to my sister on the phone, and now Megan is listing all the reasons that I won't be helping her plan our brother's wedding even though I am the only person in our family who knows how to have fun.

Not that bukkake is my idea of fun, necessarily. But I thought she'd like the baklava suggestion since our grandfather is Greek. It was an honest mistake. Slip of the tongue.

Freudian slip of the tongue, maybe.

We've moved on, and I'm only half listening to her as she yammers on about the upcoming wedding, which is still a month away, but which my entire family has been at DEFCON status for the entire engagement...in Megan's mind only. I honestly don't think Leo and Dixie, my brother and his sweet fiance, care about the wedding. They just want to go on a honeymoon, but Megan is having a particularly problematic Saturn Return this year, and it's hitting her like a mid-life crisis. Of course, she won't listen to any of my astrological advice about it, but I did slip a rose quartz into a slice in her mattress to help her relax.

"Also, your breasts are a disaster."

Well, that gets my attention. "Excuse me? What's wrong with my breasts?" I look down. I think they are rather impressive, actually. Megan is probably just jealous because she is built more like our mom, which works out pretty well for her most as the time. Being a size six, Megan has a classic beauty and lean figure. I, on the other hand, have been built like a brick house since the age of twelve. And it wasn't until I turned twenty that I learned how to use my curves to my advantage.

"The dress shop is having a really hard time getting your dress just right," Megan says.

"Well, you should've thought of that before you suggested a plunging neckline. My breasts didn't magically sprout after you chose the style."

I will admit that I am sort of the family fuck up, but I will not have my lovely lady lumps blamed for it.

She goes back to centerpieces, so I go back to web browsing.

"But I *need* to know who you're bringing, Stella." I can picture her quite clearly right now. She's in her car, probably on her way to a house showing. She's *not* fixing her lipstick because her lipstick is always already perfect. She's simultaneously planning her *someday-wedding* to Brad, how she's going to convince her executive client and his wife that the five-bedroom house on the bluff is just perfect for them despite the fact that they are moving here to downsize and only need two bedrooms, and how she's going to corral her little sister (me) into a woman of substance. At least for one day.

We all know the wedding will go off without a hitch, the exec will totally buy the house once his wife sees the view, and her sister is already a woman of substance—just not very serious substance. Thank you very much.

Anyone with a passing acquaintance with Psych 101 can diagnose classic transference. She's stressed about the fact that Brad hasn't popped the question to her, so she's obsessing about the wedding she can control. Because my brother's fiance didn't know to say no when Megan offered to plan her wedding. I'm surprised Dixie hasn't run for the hills. She must really like my brother.

Shit. Megan is still talking. "I have to know if he is going to sit at the wedding party table with us, or if he will be sitting at a guest table."

What she means is: Will he be *good enough* to sit at the family table at this ridiculously formal wedding she's planning for two people who hate formal things?

And the answer is most likely not.

I love my sister. I just love her more when she's not acting the part of Bridezilla in another woman's wedding. I am so, so tired of talking about this wedding. About dresses. Cakes. Flowers. Chair covers. Bows. Tulle. All of it.

Except maybe bukkake. I could probably talk about that for a little while longer without being bored.

One more month. If I don't kill my sister before June, it will be a miracle. She goes back to analyzing the deeper meaning of centerpieces, so I go back to web browsing. I resume half-listening status and pull up another veterinary clinic's website to research.

Dr. Anderson, my boss, wants to revamp our own veterinary clinic site, so I'm comparing our clinic to the closest metropolitan area to our small little town of Brazen Bay. I have a pretty good idea of how I want the site to look, but it never hurts to check out the city ones. More people are moving to Brazen Bay and commuting—like the househunting exec—for better or worse. We want them to feel comfortable bringing their pets here rather than the city. Or Port Jacks. Port Jacks is a college town and just gross.

"Also, he needs to wear a suit and tie. Not Dockers and a T-shirt."

"Who does?"

"Oh my God, Stella. Your date. Your date for my wedding," she screeches. "I mean Leo's wedding," she adds a little quieter.

She's really losing it.

"About my date..."

"Can you maybe bring someone who isn't in a biker gang?"

One time. I dated a biker *one* time. "Noted."

"And maybe someone whose IQ is larger than his shoe size."

My track record with men isn't great. Actually, it's awful. I tend to skip over the cerebral types in favor of eye candy with personality issues. And sometimes the big dumb ones. And the one time, a biker. In my defense, *Sons of Anarchy* was really popular.

I don't date for conversation—that's what my friends and family are for. I date guys I wouldn't want to hang around with when we're clothed. It's a problem that I understand when I'm not in the presence of a hottie. But when they are around, I usually fail to see the problem. I only see their pecs. And their forearms. And their quads. If my libido is in charge, I like them big and stupid. I've been told it's because I have commitment issues, so I'm attracted to men I would never be able to really care about.

So I tried commitment last year and it was a disaster. He ended up being the definition of toxic masculinity. Unfortunately, Cole still has a lot of people in Brazen Bay fooled. Including my sister. It doesn't matter anyway because now I'm on a self-imposed break from all men.

Including bikers. And personal trainers. And hot pizza guys.

All of them.

"Hey, Megan. I need to get back to work. Can we talk about this later? I'll call you tonight and you can tell me all the things that are wrong with my breasts and my taste in men then, okay?"

Because the conversation is going to happen whether I want it to or not, but I can at least show up armed. Wine and fuzzy slippers are the preferred armor when it comes to Megan, but even just being home would be an improvement.

I let my attention drift back to my monitor. According to the website, Dr. Rivers, one of Dr. Anderson's friends in the city, took on a new vet. I wish Doc would be like her friend and get some more help around here. Another vet would sure take some of the pressure off her. As it is, I pretty much handle her personal life scheduling or she'd neglect to have one. Leann Anderson is a fabulous animal doctor, but she totally sucks at things like eating regular meals and getting her hair cut. I have resorted to filling her Netflix queue and forcing her to take time for relaxing.

She wasn't always like this, I'm told. Back in her 20s, she was the drummer in my dad's band, Ironwing. But when they came home after their one and only world tour, she went off to veterinary school when my dad went to law school. The entire band is all boring and parental now.

I make a mental note to send a message to Dr. Rivers to ask her to talk to my boss about taking on a new vet. This guy Dr. Rivers brought on… Christopher Lockwood DVM…is an interesting character. The picture is grainy, so maybe he isn't as dorky as he appears. But, wow, look at those glasses. Thick, black frames…Clark Kent would be jealous.

"What about Cole? I bet he'd be your date," Megan asks, not ending the call as I'd hoped.

"Have you suffered a blow to your head recently, Megan? Cole and I broke up." For many, many good reasons. He has the requisite quads, but he also has the tendency to hit things that anger him. Walls mostly, but since he had me pinned up against the wall the last time he punched a hole in it, I'm not counting out the possibility that his violence is limited to inanimate objects.

"Well, he's still friends with Brad. I'm sure you guys could get along for one day. Besides, maybe you could patch things up. Wouldn't that be romantic? Getting back together at my wedding. I mean, Leo's wedding?"

"No!" I don't mean to yell, but hell-to-the-no.

Cole is not in my get-your-life-together-Stella plan. I a few months into the Year of Stella and the return of Cole would be a serious step backward. Also, I never told Megan about the hitting thing. She knows we argued, but she never knew about my wall. Nash, my landlord and friend, fixed the wall without a word, and then I heard that he and my brother had a little chat with Cole in which Cole peed his pants.

"Cole was horrible for me."

"Well, there is something to be said for bad boys."

"Bad boys, yes. Mean boys, no. Besides, what do you know about bad boys? Brad is like Saltine cracker boring."

"I don't even know what that means, but Brad is not boring. And I just don't want you to end up alone."

What Megan doesn't want is for me to embarrass her. But she'll never get her wish because no matter how I try not to be, I have always been an embarrassment to Megan. I tend to "draw attention" which is code speak for "spectacle."

For most of my life, I wanted to be like Megan. Hell, I wanted to *be* Megan. Megan is classy. Poised. Stylish. She manages to live her life without a hair out of place, a broken nail, or a bead of sweat.

I am the opposite of her in every way. I can't contain myself the way Meg does, to my sister's utter chagrin. And the harder I try to be "normal" the more I stick out and embarrass us both. She's better at enumerating all my misdeeds, but her list probably starts with the time I sent her high school boyfriend, my first crush, a love note from a secret admirer—on the back of my spelling test. Not only was my identity no longer a secret, but I misspelled "flower" by adding a "u."

Also high on her list—the time I sneezed and farted at the same time at Grandma's funeral during the moment of silence. I was sixteen.

She also probably has some things to say about the way Santa Claus terrified me well into my teens...okay, I'll be honest. Santa Claus still terrifies me. But I no longer kick him in the shin at the mall and run away.

She also never likes the perfume I wear, my clothes, my hair, the things I did to her Barbie and Ken dolls, my interest in astrology, and the way I sometimes break into song for no reason. And, of course, my taste in men.

"What you need to do is find a boyfriend. You know if you just—"

"Don't start, Megan." I'm so tired of conversations that start with "if you just."

"I want you to be happy. Snagging a man isn't brain surgery, you know. You're a great girl. If you just—"

Desperate to cut her off, I blurt out, "I'm seeing somebody!"

Why did I say that?

God, now what? Damage control is key here. Because Megan is a cunning opponent in the game of wits. Like any good salesperson, she knows her prey better than they do.

"It's new. I haven't told anyone yet because we're ...trying to...uh...take it slow. You know, nurture it a little."

I want to hit my head on the desk. *Why can't you control your mouth?* Stupid. Stupid and nothing good this way comes. I know

Megan won't let it go. She is going to be all over me like her sorority sisters at a Juicy Couture outlet store.

"Who is he?"

I crumple paper over the mic on my phone. "What? What? Megan, you're breaking up. Are you going through a tunnel?"

"Nice try."

Think, Stella. "I told you that we're keeping this on the down-low for now. He's just out of a bad relationship, too." That seems plausible, right? For this guy who I'm completely making up to be nursing a broken heart?

"At least tell me his name."

I look around the reception area for a lifeline, my eyes settling on my monitor and Dr. Rivers' website. "Christopher. His name is Christopher."

"Oh, I like that name. Where did you meet him?"

Fantastic. She likes that name. That must mean he's a good boyfriend if Megan likes his name. "The internet?" That isn't a lie exactly.

"The internet? Seriously, Stella?"

God it's like my sister is stuck in the '90s. "Yes, the internet. It's this thing where you can communicate with people all over the world through a little box in your house or sometimes your phone." Wait until I tell her about the dating apps. The idea of swiping will horrify her.

"Funny. What's he like? Where is he from?"

I look at the fuzzy picture, tilting my head sideways and then back. I can't tell her that he's grainy or grayscale. "He's kind of serious." Nobody else would look that earnest in thick glasses. "But he's great with animals." Probably. "He lives in the city."

"Well, he must be a vet then, if you know he's good with animals."

"Or maybe, Nancy Drew, he's just an animal lover." I check the time, lunch is almost over. "I really have to go. Appointments start soon."

"Okay...but call me later."

"Right." Right after I get that lobotomy I need.

Get *So Wrong It's Right*[3] from your favorite vendor today!

---

3. *https://books2read.com/sowrongitsright*

Also by Brill Harper

Blue Collar Bad Boys
Bounced: A Blue Collar Bad Boys Book
Nailed: A Blue Collar Bad Boys Book
Drilled: A Blue Collar Bad Boys Book
Wrecked: A Blue Collar Bad Boys Book
Laid: A Blue Collar Bad Boys Book
Tagged
Plowed
Bucked: A Blue Collar Bad Boys Book
Banged: A Blue Collar Bad Boys Book
Tapped: A Blue Collar Bad Boy Book

It's Complicated
All Together
All at Once

Love in Brazen Bay
Wrong Number Text
The Right Stuff
So Wrong It's Right

Don't Get Me Wrong

Standalone
Dirty Jobs: a Blue Collar Bad Boys Collection
Notch on His Bedpost
Honeymoon With The Prince:: A Modern Day Fairy Tale
Good Girl

Watch for more at https://brillharper.com.

www.ingramcontent.com/pod-product-compliance
Lightning Source LLC
Chambersburg PA
CBHW051214160726
47994CB00002B/604